RADIO DARK

RADIO DARK

A NOVEL

SHANE HINTON

BURROW PRESS | ORLANDO, FL

Published by Burrow Press
PO Box 533709
Orlando, FL 32853
burrowpress.com

Book design: Ryan Rivas
Cover image: epatrician
Manatee icon: bubaone
Manatee illustraion: ilbusca

ISBN: 978-1-941681-60-2
LCCN: 2018965845

Distributed by Itasca Books
orders@itascabooks.com

Burrow Press is supported in part by its subscribers and:

ALSO BY SHANE HINTON

Pinkies: stories
We Can't Help It If We're From Florida (editor)

PRAISE FOR *PINKIES*

"If Kafka got it on with Flannery O'Connor, *Pinkies* would be their love child." **– LIDIA YUKNAVITCH** author of *The Book of Joan*

"Shane Hinton's *Pinkies* is weird, and it is wonderful. This debut collection–in which the everyday is always extraordinary–reminds me of fiction by Joy Williams and Mary Robison, and also of movies by Charlie Kaufman. If that sounds like ridiculously high praise, then good: *Pinkies* deserves it."
– BROCK CLARKE author of *The Price of the Haircut*

"A remarkable new young American writer."
– *MIKHAIL IOSSEL* author of *Notes from Cyberground*

PRAISE FOR *WE CAN'T HELP IT...*

"As hot and wild and dangerous as our beloved (or is it bedeviled?) state, itself. While no book could ever fully explain the mysteries of today's Sunshine State, this smart chorus of varied and brilliant voices comes as close as any I've read."
– LAUREN GROFF author of *Florida*

"As weird and funny and beautiful and unnerving as you might expect from some of our state's best writers."
– KAREN RUSSELL author of *Swamplandia!*

"A heartfelt, complex counter to all those #FloridaMan jokes."
– KIRKUS REVIEWS

PRAISE FOR *RADIO DARK*

"A book about what it means to own and live inside a failing physical body, as well as a failing community body."
— **KRISTEN ARNETT** author of *Mostly Dead Things*

"A raw and propulsive novel that shivers with life and shimmers with hope." — **MEREDITH ALLING** author of *Sing the Song*

"Shane Hinton has a hold on a post-apocalyptic setting in a way that would make the author of the Book of Revelation proud. *Radio Dark* melds *The Road* with *Mad Max* with *The Walking Dead*. Welcome to the wondrous world of Shane Hinton."
— **GEORGE SINGLETON** author of *Staff Picks*

"Questions I asked myself while reading *Radio Dark*: Is Florida anyone's proper home anymore? Are the punishments we deserve and our darkest aspirations one and the same? If we lost our voices and hands, would it help us know our souls? Do burning orange trees really smell like cheap candy? Is the whole purpose of naming your soul's disease to prove you have a soul? This book is the hoarse, rasping warning of a doom that feels deserved, of a slow-moving apocalypse that's both shocking and also a logical conclusion for an age of willful ignorance and spiritual paucity."
— **JOHN BRANDON** author of *Further Joy*

"Hinton's understated yet sharp prose pushes us over the edge into a quietly spiraling horror. An unforgettable read."
— **STEPH POST** author of *Miraculum*

"Morbidly surreal. Hinton's apocalyptic vision is rendered tenderly in this sadly-beautiful book. He compels us to listen for truth in the crackling jumble of noise and find hope in pockets of silence."
— **JASON OCKERT** author of *Wasp Box*

for Snooty

1

Memphis did his grocery shopping in the middle of the day, when the aisles were uncrowded and shoppers walked lazily between displays, taking too long to eye weekly specials, putting items into their carts and then taking them out again. He pushed a cart with a crooked wheel past an older couple standing in front of a selection of taco seasoning.

"I think it was the yellow one," the man said, his finger tapping his chin.

"I'll call him," the woman said, taking a cell phone from her purse.

"Don't bother him. Get the yellow one."

"I'll just call him. It's no bother."

Memphis put a jar of pickled jalapeños in his cart. As he turned the corner, the couple was still facing each other silently, the woman holding a phone to her ear, the man watching her with his arms crossed.

In the dairy aisle, Memphis stood behind an overweight woman in a flowered dress. She shifted gently from foot to foot, indecisive. He could see the milk through the freezer door but couldn't reach around her, so he tapped her on the shoulder. "Excuse me," he said. The woman didn't respond.

Memphis leaned to look into her face and saw her eyes moving rapidly from side to side. Her jaw tensed and released. Memphis stepped back.

"Over here, boys." A manager in a red vest led two teenage employees around the corner. He put his hand on the woman's shoulder. "I'm back," he said to her. "I've got two stock boys here with me. We're going to make you more comfortable."

Memphis watched the woman's face in the glass freezer door.

"We just happen to be in need of additional help at the moment," the manager said to the woman. One of the boys wheeled a dolly closer to her.

"Excuse us, sir," the manager said to Memphis. "We'll have this cleaned up in just a minute."

One of the boys positioned the dolly directly behind the woman's heels as the other one knelt down beside her. "I'm going to move your foot," he said, and lifted her foot, placing it on the dolly. The woman's eyes continued to move quickly from side to side. He moved her other foot onto the dolly and then stood up, taking her hand in his. "How are you doing? Is there anything I can do to make you more comfortable?"

The woman seemed to speak. It sounded like air escaping a tire.

"That's fine, that's fine," the manager said. "Tilt her back, boys, gently now. She's getting off balance."

The stock boys leaned the dolly back, bending their legs and squaring up against the woman's weight as she angled away from the refrigerated cases.

"Over by the cleaning supplies," the manager said, "on the endcap." The manager turned to Memphis and handed him a coupon for one dollar off whole-wheat rotini. "I'm sorry for the delay, sir. Please take this for your inconvenience."

Memphis backed away without getting milk. As he approached the cash register, he saw they had placed the woman in front of a display of glass cleaner and hung a sign around her neck reading "Special of the Week: 25% off." Her eyes shifted from side to side, her mouth silently opening and closing, fingers twitching, knees shaking. The flowers on her dress looked withered and dry.

•

"Blessed are the shallow of lung, for their every breath is a slip nearer the abyss. Blessed are the restricted of diaphragm, for their muscles spasm in the presence of the Lord. Blessed are the hoarse, for their rasping is the sound of God, and their sore throats shall be his persecuted messengers, forever and ever, amen."

Memphis mopped the lobby of the radio station as the pastor took off his headset and opened the studio door. As always, five members of his congregation stood around the coffee table in the waiting area, listening to his nightly sermon in a tight circle, holding hands, heads bowed and eyes closed. Without speaking, the members of the prayer circle lifted their heads and followed the pastor out the glass door of the radio station toward a small church bus in the side parking lot, leaving muddy tracks on Memphis' freshly mopped floor. A public service announcement played over the speakers in the lobby.

Memphis' favorite show was up next. It had been on the air for almost twenty years. The DJ played upbeat music for people who worked the graveyard shift. Memphis ran his mop over the muddy footprints as the DJ's voice came over the speakers.

"This one's for the truck drivers. Have another cup of coffee and try not to tap your toes on the gas pedal. It's going to be another beautiful Tuesday morning out there, sunrise at six forty-two, and it should be a stunner. Lots of particulate matter in the air, as they say, so keep your eyes on the road and your ears on the radio."

After he finished mopping, Memphis straightened the desks of the news crew who would be in just before dawn. He emptied their trash cans and pushed in their chairs. He sprayed disinfectant on the surfaces of their desks, careful to avoid stacks of papers and manila folders. He wiped down the windows that looked out over the parking lot, where his rusty silver sedan and the DJ's small green pickup sat under the only streetlight. On the window, his cleaning chemicals fogged and cleared. Condensation from the air conditioning gathered and dripped down the glass in small streams. It was the middle of summer and hot, even at night.

Memphis finished his shift before the DJ's show was over. He waved to him on his way out. From the other side of the soundproof glass, the DJ smiled and waved back while reading a public service announcement about brain-eating amoebas. "Remember," he said, "stagnant water may seem warm and inviting, but it's not worth the risk."

·

The streets of Memphis' town had been orange groves when he was a boy. He remembered as, one by one, the groves were bulldozed to make room for neighborhoods, for the people from up North, finally tired of the long winters, to settle into their respiratory diseases and neurological disorders. When a developer bulldozed an orange grove, they would burn all of the trees. Memphis remembered great piles of them, stacked up to the sky and blazing. He remembered the sweetness in the air on those days, the way it smelled like oranges but not really, more like cheap candy.

Slowly the town filled up with strip malls and gas stations. The streets were expanded from two lanes to four, then six. The new houses were spaced respectful distances from each other, giving families just enough room to feel like landowners, a little space to take pictures of and fill up with swimming pools and play sets.

Young families bought the new houses, then bought newer ones when the new houses weren't new anymore. Memphis' family lived on the edge of town, which stayed the edge of town even after the development boom consumed all the woodland between their house and the closest grocery store. His parents had hoped to sell and capitalize on the growth, but they had been smokers for too long and the cancer grew quicker than the real estate market.

The house Memphis had bought with his fiancé was small. His whole neighborhood was full of similar houses. Two- and three-bedroom places, laid out awkwardly, the living rooms too close to the kitchen, the bathrooms too close to both. The day they had signed the contract his fiancé had stood in the living room and stretched her arms out, smiling wider than he'd ever seen her smile. They were homeowners. This validated something that he couldn't exactly point to.

When Memphis got home from the radio station, he sat in front of the upright piano he had taken from his parents' house before the foreclosure. He stretched his fingers out and let them hover over the keys, imagining the chords he could play, but dropped them back into his lap and rubbed the coarse material of his work slacks instead. His uniform shirt was open and he fidgeted with the lowest button, poking it through its hole and then popping it back out.

The songs of his childhood were beginning to fade. He could remember pieces of the melodies, parts of lyrics, but they were becoming indistinct from one another. He closed his eyes and stretched his fingers out again, then lifted them to his face and rubbed his eyes. The calluses on his palms were rough, and his hands smelled like disinfectant. He inhaled deeply.

The streetlights outside his window flickered off and then on and then off again as sunrise broke over the horizon. He looked around at the empty house. Six weeks earlier, his fiancé had rented a moving truck while he was at work. When he came home, most of the expensive items in the house were missing. She left a note on the refrigerator: "I might have a brain inflammation." The only large pieces of furniture she left behind were the couch, the dining table, the twin bed from the spare bedroom, and the piano. All of it looked out of context and unfamiliar now. It was like being in someone else's house.

Memphis took his shirt off and stood in front of the bathroom mirror. He leaned in to look at his face. A small pimple was beginning to form in the corner of his mouth. He squeezed the white bulb between his two pointer fingers and it erupted onto the surface of the mirror. He closed his eyes. An ache lingered where the pimple had been, but the pressure was released.

He turned his attention to a sore behind his earlobe. It was scabbed over and inflamed. Pressing his ear down to the side of his head, he dug at the sore with the tip of his fingernail, picking against the edge of the scab until it pulled away from his skin. He let the scab drop into the sink and looked at the tip of his finger, covered in blood, before holding it under his nose and inhaling. The chemical smell of disinfectant mixed with the smell of blood. He turned on the hot water and rubbed his hands together under the stream.

It was seven in the morning. He lay down in bed with his inflamed ear against the cool pillow and stared at the sunlight leaking around the edges of his black curtains.

•

The pastor's church was just around the corner from Memphis' house. It was a white building with a modest steeple. It was called First Elemental Church of Christ the Soft-Spoken. Every evening at sundown a member of the congregation blew a single long trumpet blast. Memphis was sitting at his dining table drinking coffee when he heard the trumpet. He looked at the clock. His shift started in fifteen minutes.

On the way to the station, Memphis turned his radio off and kept his windows down. It was a community station with a limited broadcast range. Its signal barely reached the suburbs. The limited broadcast power made him feel better about being so close to the tower every night. He sometimes worried about the effects on his health, and occasionally convinced himself he could feel the radio waves vibrating in his chest, spawning cancer cells in organs he could point to but not name. As he got closer to the station, he reached up and scratched at the pimple in the corner of his mouth. He knew he should leave it alone, but the scab came off and he pressed the collar of his shirt against it to stop the bleeding.

The station's tower jutted from the top of the building and rose over the tops of the shotgun houses lining the street. As Memphis approached, he leaned forward to see the top of it through his windshield. It was the smallest tower in town but it still seemed impossibly tall. He liked to imagine climbing it, what the city would look like from up there.

When Memphis got to the radio station, a white van was parked next to the church bus in the parking lot. Black letters on the side read "FCC." Federal agents had the authority to visit the station at any time, but during his two years as a janitor Memphis had never seen an inspection. He turned the car off and sat for a moment in silence, pressing the collar of his shirt against the corner of his mouth until it no longer left spots on the fabric. Through his open windows he could hear someone yelling, "Federal Communications Commission. Open up!" He got out of the car and walked to the front of the station, where a woman was banging on the glass door. Her free hand clutched a clipboard and a lit cigarette was wedged between her fingers. Inside the lobby, just on the other side of the door, the pastor's congregation held hands around the coffee table. A spread of entertainment magazines sat undisturbed on the table in front of them.

The woman turned to Memphis. "Do you work here?" she asked, looking down at his name tag.

"Sorry," Memphis said, gesturing to the congregation in

the lobby, "they don't talk." He swiped his keycard and held the door open. The woman dropped her cigarette and crushed it beneath the toe of her shoe.

"Memphis?" she asked, tapping his name tag with her pointer finger. "I'm Cincinnati. Let's get started."

Inside the lobby Cincinnati immediately began taking notes. She circled around the congregation, looking closely at each member's face before moving to the next. "Obstruction of a federal agent," Cincinnati said. "Disrupting the process of a legally required inspection. Endangering the public safety by interfering with an unscheduled emergency broadcast test." She scribbled on her clipboard. "Anything to say for yourselves?"

The congregation moved their mouths silently, eyes closed and heads lowered as always.

"You can expect a letter outlining these infractions." She looked up at the glass separating the studio from the lobby. Inside, the pastor spoke into the microphone with his eyes closed. His voice came through the lobby speakers.

"And what is the way to the Kingdom of Heaven? Loud mufflers and heavy bass? I'm no expert, dear listeners, but I don't think the Lord our God calls to us from clouds of exhaust. I don't think the Son of Man beckons from the back of a club filled with half-deaf dancers. We must plug our ears if we want to hear the sounds of Heaven, we must be so quiet that we hear the blood flowing through our veins, so quiet that we can make out the ringing of our poor decisions, the aftermath of our mistakes."

Cincinnati made notes on her clipboard. "How long does his show last?" she asked Memphis.

Memphis looked up at the clock, though he already knew the answer. "He just started."

•

At home in bed, Memphis lay on his back looking through the paperwork Cincinnati left with him after her inspection was complete. The overhead light bled through the forms, making Cincinnati's handwritten letters seem thin and disconnected from each other. She had walked through the entire studio, pointing out pieces of equipment that Memphis had never noticed. There were important-looking black boxes covered in green and red lights tucked away in small rooms where Memphis had been specifically instructed not to touch anything. Cincinnati had touched things, though. She pressed buttons and initiated diagnostic cycles. She swept her finger through dust on the tops of the machines and showed it to Memphis. "Aren't you the janitor?" she asked. Memphis hung his head and touched the scab behind his ear. Now, as he lay in bed, he wished he had come up with something more to tell her. Cincinnati was beautiful in a way he didn't know people could be beautiful, like an empty seat in the back of a crowded restaurant.

The sun was coming up but Memphis couldn't sleep. His chest was tight with regret. He pulled his clothes back on and went out for a walk.

Memphis' neighborhood was full of houses that looked almost the same. A few blocks from his house the street became a dirt road that ran through a diseased orange grove. Withered orange trees in various stages of dying lined either side of the path. The fruit no longer turned the color it was supposed to. Oranges hung from branches, half-green and half-yellow. Memphis picked one, looked at it, then threw it out into the grove. He couldn't hear where it landed.

He walked in the loose sand until he came to a kidney-shaped pond. At the water's edge, a girl with an orange plastic bucket in one hand and a fish net in the other knelt in front of a hole. Tiny silver fish flopped around in the drying mud at the bottom of the hole.

"Those fish need water," Memphis said.

The girl looked up at Memphis, then back down at the hole. She picked up a fish that had stopped moving and held it up to her face. "This fish is dead," she said as she tossed it back into the pond. It floated on the surface of the water. She picked up another. "This fish is dead," she said, tossing it into the pond, picking up another. "This fish is dead, and this fish is dead, and this fish is dead," she said as their mouths opened and closed and opened again, their tiny chests expanding and compressing, then staying compressed.

2

At the radio station, Memphis parked next to a green sedan. A man stood by the driver-side door with his arms at his sides. As Memphis got closer, he recognized the man as one of the station's news reporters. The man shifted his weight from foot to foot. Car keys dangled from his right hand, looking as if they might drop from his loose grip.

Memphis approached the reporter slowly. "Everything okay?" he asked. He guided the man's hand toward the handle of the car and pushed the key into the keyhole. The reporter held onto the keys but made no effort to turn them in the lock. Memphis put his hand on top of the reporter's and gently twisted, releasing the lock, then opened the door. He guided the man into the driver's seat, smoothed out his red tie before buckling him in. Memphis shut the door but the man just stared forward with his hands in his lap.

Inside, the DJ read a public service announcement. "It's Lyme season again, folks, which means it's time to avoid high grass and be constantly aware of your own skin. Get familiar with your bumps and folds. Ticks seek comfort in small spaces."

Memphis started his cleaning routine but found himself glancing at the glass doors of the station, hoping Cincinnati would be there. The DJ went back to playing songs, country and upbeat, that had Memphis sweeping in rhythm. He swept under the news reporters' desks and in the hallway where they kept the coffee pot. A pile of dust accumulated at the end of his broom, mixed together with scraps of paper and pieces of styrofoam cups. In the middle of a song about sitting on the bank of the river and watching dead limbs float out to sea, the DJ broke in with an announcement.

"We've just gotten word that area schools will be closed tomorrow. All high schools will host vaccination centers and residents are encouraged to arrive early."

The DJ turned the music back on and met Memphis in the hallway. "Did you get the shot?" he asked, rolling up his sleeve to show Memphis a welt in the crook of his elbow. Its red center stood out from his pale, freckled skin.

Memphis shook his head

"It's getting weird out there," the DJ said. "People have been calling in all night and just breathing into the phone." He pointed through the soundproof glass to the phone in the studio. All six lines were lit up and flashing. "I can't even get them to hang up."

Memphis looked out the window into the parking lot. The green sedan was still there, its lights off, its windows rolled up. He could make out the shape of the reporter's head in the driver's seat.

•

Memphis finished his shift at the radio station and drove straight to the high school. The shoulders of the small residential streets around the school were lined with cars. He had to park a couple blocks away and walk. In the front parking lot of the school, a large blue and white striped tent billowed in the wind. Outside the tent a crowd waited in line. A woman with a white CDC badge gave Memphis a form to complete and directed him to a line of healthy-looking adults. Another line, entering the opposite side of the tent, was for families with children. It began to rain lightly and a CDC representative walked down the line handing out cheap umbrellas for the parents to hold over their kids to keep them dry. Memphis examined the faces of the people around him, trying to pick out whom he had seen at the store or around the neighborhood, but he recognized no one. The crowds stared at the ground or talked quietly on phones.

Memphis' line moved slowly. At the door to the tent another woman in a white uniform took the form he had filled out. "Any allergies to medication?" she asked.

Memphis shook his head.

"Family history of mental illness?"

He shook his head again.

"Tell me about your professional ambitions. Where do you see yourself in five years?"

"Doing what I do now, probably." Memphis looked down at his feet.

"Do you fight the urge to stay in bed when you wake up?"

The white parking lines on the pavement seemed out of place inside the tent. Memphis tried to imagine the tent filled up with cars. He looked back up at the woman. "Huh?"

"How long would you say it takes you to go from asleep to fully dressed on an average work day?"

"Ten minutes, I guess."

The woman looked at him over the top of her glasses. "You guess?"

Memphis nodded.

The woman pointed to a padded table and Memphis sat on top of a sheet of sterile paper that crinkled beneath him. Rain smacked the roof of the tent, and he looked up to see if it was leaking.

"Roll up your sleeve," the woman said. "This is going to hurt."

Memphis held his breath and looked away. He watched the shadows of heavy raindrops hitting the canvas, his eyes chasing them back and forth across the blue and white striped surface. Wind shook the walls of the tent and the woman leaned over him and said, "Ready?" He closed his eyes and the needle went into his arm with a pinch. When she injected the fluid the pain was so intense he pulled away involuntarily, causing the needle to move under his skin and feel like it was carving out a hole inside his arm.

"All done," the woman said, taping a piece of gauze over the injection site. "Give your paperwork to the woman at the desk on your way out."

As he walked out of the tent, Memphis looked into the face of a young girl, no more than seven or eight, seated on a padded table with tears in her eyes. A man in white handed her a foam ball and told her to squeeze. The little girl looked back at Memphis, and when the needle went into her arm she screamed so loud that everyone in the tent turned to look.

•

By the time Memphis got back to his house, lightning was flashing all around. He left his wet shoes by the front door and went straight to the bedroom. He needed sleep, but when he went to shut the blinds, he noticed a figure standing at the end of the street. Between the rivulets of water pouring down the glass, he could barely make out the girl with the orange bucket. She was wearing the same clothes she'd had on the day before. Lightning struck so close that the thunder was almost simultaneous and, without stopping to think, Memphis ran out into the storm.

His bare feet splashed through deep puddles as he made his way toward the girl. When he reached her, lightning struck again, close enough that he could feel the thunder in his chest. The girl didn't blink. Her orange bucket was overflowing with rainwater. Minnows swam in frantic circles inside it. Memphis reached out and touched the girl's shoulder, shaking her slightly. Three or four of the tiny fish tumbled out onto the street and washed into the gutter and down the storm drain. "You have to get inside," Memphis said. "Where is your house?"

Memphis looked up and down the street at the nearly identical houses. Most of the cars were in their driveways, but no one was standing on any of the porches looking for the girl, no one stood in any of the windows looking out at them. "Okay," Memphis said. "Come with me." He pulled on the girl's arm but she didn't budge. "Come on. I'll make you some soup." He waved his hand in front of the girl's face, but she didn't respond, so he picked her up and put her over his shoulder. The orange bucket swung against his ribs as he ran toward his house, looking in each of the windows as he passed.

The girl was heavier than he expected. His knees felt weak. He set the girl down in the entryway of his house and dialed 911. A recorded voice answered and said, "We are currently experiencing high call volume. Please try again later." The girl stood where Memphis had placed her, drops of water falling from her long hair and soaking into the carpet at her feet.

3

The girl with the orange bucket had been standing for more than six hours when Memphis realized that she might like to sit down. He pulled the girl to the kitchen table, put a bowl in front of her and filled it with cereal and milk, then put a spoon in her right hand and set the hand on the table. She gripped the spoon but just barely, and Memphis could see that if he pulled it, the spoon would easily come free.

Memphis sat and watched the girl from across the kitchen table. Her nostrils flared, her chest rose and fell, but she just stared straight ahead.

After the rain stopped, Memphis tried again to get her to speak: What street do you live on? What do your parents do for work? Do you have any brothers or sisters? Is your fishing license up to date? What's your least favorite subject in school?

Her eyes moved, widened, but she didn't answer.

When the horn from the pastor's church signaled sundown, Memphis got into his car and headed to the station. At the intersection near his house, he sat behind a long line of cars as the traffic light cycled through green, then yellow, then red, without any of the vehicles moving. Memphis eased around the cars in the oncoming lane, looking at the drivers as he passed. They all stared straight ahead with their hands on their steering wheels. He pulled carefully through the intersection, but as far as he could see, his was the only car moving.

•

The white FCC van was in the parking lot again. Inside the station, Cincinnati paced in front of the receptionist's desk, holding her clipboard to her chest. The DJ stood by the studio door, waiting for his shift with his hands in his pockets. The pastor's congregation stood nearby in their usual positions, holding hands around the coffee table. In the center of the table a magazine promised "50 Ideas for a Quiet Night In."

"Maintain lines of communication," Cincinnati said as she counted on her fingers. "Ensure that the nation's airwaves are protected and appropriately utilized. My name is Cincinnati and my badge number is 46138 and I have no children. My name is Cincinnati and my badge number is 46138. My name is Cincinnati and I have no children. Evacuate major population centers."

She looked up, noticing Memphis for the first time. "You're here," she said, surprised. She reached out and touched the welt where he had received the vaccination. "You got the shot," she said. "How do you feel? Fever? Irritability?"

Memphis shook his head. He touched the sore at the corner of his mouth, then the welt. Both were covered over with a layer of dried pus. He picked gently at the corner of his mouth until the scab came loose, then stuck out his tongue to lick the blood away.

The DJ pulled hard on the studio door, but it was locked

from the inside. He looked up at the clock nervously. His show was scheduled to start in minutes.

Inside the studio, the pastor stood in front of the microphone with his eyes closed. "Can you hear it, listeners? Our time has come. The cars idling outside are running out of gas. Their batteries are draining, their stereos are shutting down. Their turn signals are slowing. Their air conditioners are giving up. This is our era, the era of silence, and I never lie to my listeners, my imperiled brothers and sisters. When I speak it is only in anticipation of my own silence, it is only as the bird speaks before the hurricane, alighting from the branch and leaving its nest behind as its offspring feel the first winds of the storm before it blows them to the wet ground. When I speak it is in the service of a sound we don't deserve, a sound we can't hear with our earthly ears. Pierce your eardrums now, listeners, and sit at the right hand of God."

Cincinnati banged on the soundproof glass and held her notes up in front of her. "You need to read this on the air," she yelled, but the pastor continued to preach with his eyes closed until well after his allotted time. When he finally stopped, he walked out of the studio without acknowledging Memphis, Cincinnati or the DJ. The pastor took the hand of one member of his congregation and led her toward the exit. The rest of the congregation, linked by their hands, followed them out the front door. Memphis watched the pastor place each member in the church bus one by one, buckling their seatbelts, then shutting the doors.

Cincinnati and Memphis and the DJ stood in the lobby, looking at the empty sound booth. The light above the door read "On Air."

"I don't think we should be here," the DJ said.

Memphis and Cincinnati watched the girl with the orange bucket from the couch across the room. The cereal in front of her was bloated, the milk curdled. The TV was turned to a news network, but the anchor on-screen had been staring straight into the camera without speaking since they'd turned on the TV. Beneath her face, a crawl reported breaking news: "64 confirmed dead from gas explosion in western Pennsylvania * * * Major failure of the electric grid in the Southeast * * * Hurricane season expected to top predicted storm frequency * * * Red tide on the Atlantic coast causes massive die-off."

Cincinnati picked up the remote control and turned off the TV. Outside, a car door slammed. The DJ pulled back the curtain on the living room window. Across the street, a family loaded suitcases into a minivan.

Memphis hurried outside and approached the family. A mother and father were buckling two children into the rear seats. The kids stared down at video game systems on their laps. As Memphis got closer, he could see that the screens were blank. "Excuse me," he said.

The mother put up her hand. "Stay back," she said. She cradled a small statue of an angel, her fingers wrapped tight around its wings.

"Where are you going?" Memphis asked.

The father crossed his arms over his chest. "There's no one left."

"We've got a government agent," Memphis said, gesturing to Cincinnati, who was standing in the doorway of Memphis' house.

The father walked closer to Memphis and whispered, "The kids haven't eaten in two days. Do you know anything?"

Memphis shook his head.

"We're going to find help. I can't just sit here and watch them starve to death," the father said. He walked around the van, got in the driver's seat, and started the ignition.

The mother checked the boys' seatbelts before sliding the door shut and climbing in the front seat. "Take care of our flowers," she said.

The van drove away and Memphis looked at the front of their house. In neat rows under the windows, beds of red, yellow, and orange flowers bloomed in repeating patterns. It was the peak of growing season. With proper care, the flowers would continue to thrive for months before fall came.

•

The DJ snored in the recliner as Memphis and Cincinnati sat on the edge of the bed. Memphis picked through a box of keepsakes left behind by his fiancé. Cincinnati read out loud from a field manual she had retrieved from her van: "If a natural or man-made disaster threatens the fabric of society, it is a core responsibility of the field agent to both maintain and expand the communications infrastructure of the nation. If the communications infrastructure has been irreparably damaged, the field agent should make use of locally available resources to ensure that a continuous emergency broadcast may be established. It is the responsibility of the field agent to coordinate with other government agencies as to what this broadcast should entail. In the event that no other government agencies are reachable, the field agent should use her intuition to create a practical and reassuring message to the public in an effort to reconstruct the social contract."

Memphis found an unpaid parking ticket made out to his fiancé. In the comments section, the parking enforcement officer had written, "Owner combative when confronted. Multiple complaints from business owners re: lack of customer parking."

Cincinnati closed the field manual and moved closer to Memphis, reading the ticket over his shoulder. "Do you miss her?" she asked.

Memphis nodded.

"Do you have any pictures?"

Memphis flipped through the box, but there were no pictures. "She must have taken them," he said.

Cincinnati put her hand on top of Memphis'. "I want to show you something." She led him outside to her van. "Come in here," she said, climbing inside, keeping her head low so it wouldn't hit the ceiling.

The walls of the van were lined with equipment. "What does it all do?" Memphis asked, looking at the dials and switches labeled with abbreviations.

"Locates unauthorized signals. Monitors radio traffic that might interfere with necessary public safety infrastructure, like air traffic control, police radio—that kind of thing."

Memphis gently touched a silver knob. It was cold. Cincinnati put her hand on top of his. "Turn it," she said, putting pressure on his fingers with hers. Together, they turned the knob and the display on the equipment came to life. A digital readout showed a radio frequency, and a meter below it moved slightly up and down.

"There's still somebody broadcasting," she said. "I found

it this morning. Probably unlicensed. Someone still wants to make noise."

Memphis looked at the orange light of the meter, then at Cincinnati's eyes. He had never been close enough to notice that her eyes were both green and brown. Cincinnati reached up and touched the sore at the corner of his mouth.

"Does it hurt?" she asked.

Memphis shook his head.

The inside of the van was hot. There were no clouds out to block the sun. Cincinnati pulled off her shirt, then put Memphis' hands on her chest. Soon all their clothes were piled in the corner of the van and Memphis was on top of her. She kissed the corner of his mouth, where the sore had again scabbed over. When he pressed his body into hers, their heads bumped into the stacks of equipment, making the meters jump.

4

The power went off just after sunset. Memphis took the food from the refrigerator and lined it up on the counter. A jug of milk, a jar of pickles, a carton of ice cream. He lit a candle and placed it on the kitchen table. The flickering light made the girl with the orange bucket look like she might be smiling.

The DJ ate ice cream out of the carton with a large spoon. "So it begins," he said, "or ends. One or the other."

They sat in the living room until the small candle sputtered as the flame touched the wax and the sharp smell of smoke filled the room. "I'll just sleep on the couch," the DJ said. In the dark, Memphis ran his fingers along the wall as he stumbled toward the bedroom. Cincinnati followed, and they felt their way to Memphis' small bed.

Memphis couldn't sleep. The night was hot, and without air conditioning the small room began to smell like sweat. He opened the window and mosquitoes buzzed against the screen, trying to get in. He touched Cincinnati's back as she slept, and she grunted and rolled away from him. He rubbed his eyes and wondered what time it was. The clocks were off and the moon was high, but wasn't the moon sometimes high at different times of the night? He didn't know very much about the moon.

In the morning Memphis went outside before the DJ or Cincinnati woke up. There were no sounds other than birds and crickets. At the end of the street, in the cul-de-sac, Memphis saw someone moving from driveway to driveway. He started toward the figure, walking barefoot through the dewy grass. When he got closer he could see it was the pastor.

"It's you," the pastor said. "Do you live in the neighborhood?" The pastor had a stack of leaflets in his hand. He stuck one beneath the windshield wiper of a parked car and moved on, talking to Memphis over his shoulder. "I've never seen you at our services."

Memphis followed beside him, trying to read the front of the leaflet. "I'm not very religious," Memphis said.

"My advice would be to get very religious," the pastor said. "Have one of these." He handed Memphis a leaflet. On the cover was a cartoon drawing of a man wearing headphones with his eyes closed and his mouth open in a scream. The title of the pamphlet was "The Devil Rides on Sound Waves and How We Can Defeat Him With our Imperfect Ears."

"Give it a read," the pastor said. "Your right hand knows not what your left hand does."

•

Cincinnati parked the FCC van on the curb in front of the radio station. There was no traffic and therefore no need to follow traffic laws. Memphis climbed out of the passenger seat and swiped his keycard in the front door. The electronic lock didn't beep. Memphis knew the power was out but had still expected it to be on when he flipped the light switch that morning, pushed the power button on his TV, plugged in his electric razor. He pulled on the handle but the door didn't budge.

Cincinnati leaned against the glass, cupping her hands around her eyes. "It's too dark inside," she said. "I can't see anything."

"Watch out," Memphis said. Cincinnati backed up and Memphis began to kick at the glass door. He kicked with his heel until it shattered, then scraped his flashlight around the edges of the frame and stepped through, careful to avoid the jagged points of broken glass still clinging to the sides, turning on his flashlight as he entered. He held out his hand and helped Cincinnati through the door.

The lobby of the radio station was trashed. Pages ripped from the receptionist's desk calendar were scattered on the floor. The magazines on the coffee table were opened, their subscription cards torn in half. Inside the sound booth, the microphones had been smashed to pieces. The CD player and turntable were hanging off the desk from their plugs. Cincinnati picked up a mangled microphone and held it in the beam of her flashlight. "Oh God," she said, dropping the microphone. "The transmitter."

Cincinnati hurried to a small room near the back of the station. Memphis followed close behind. As she opened the door, she gasped. Memphis looked in over her shoulder. All of the equipment inside the room had been destroyed. Stacks of servers were toppled on the floor, the metal shelves they had sat on twisted and broken beneath them. She reached out and touched the broken glass cover of one of the machines, tracing the edge with her finger.

Memphis put his hand on her shoulder. Cincinnati held her finger up to her face, shining the flashlight on her hand. The broken glass had opened a cut on the tip of her finger. "I couldn't even feel it," she said. Blood ran down her arm and dripped onto the tile floor. Memphis watched the drops collect at their feet, thinking, suddenly, about mopping.

They left the station, shards of glass crunching under their shoes. Cincinnati slid open the rear door of the van and pulled a thick black binder out of a plastic box, flipped to the middle, and started running her finger down the pages. The pages fluttered as she turned them, faster and faster, until she stopped, tapped her finger on a block of text, and climbed into the driver's seat.

Cincinnati drove back to Memphis' house without speaking. The streets were full of cars parked at awkward angles, their seats occupied by motionless drivers and passengers. She took corners fast, weaving in and out of the oncoming lanes, driving on the sidewalk when she had to, avoiding the mass of glass and metal that flashed in the midday sun.

Cincinnati parked the van on the lawn and threw open the door. Memphis followed her inside his house and found her standing next to the girl with the orange bucket. She took the girl's hand and elbow and guided her to her feet. The girl swayed slightly under her own weight. Cincinnati lifted the girl's arms above her head and let go. The girl stayed in that position, her palms together as in prayer.

Cincinnati picked up the binder she'd pulled from a box in the back of the van. It was labeled "Plans For Emergency Reestablishment." She flipped to a page near the middle, then traced the lines with her finger as she read.

Memphis picked up a can of tuna from the counter. The

pile of food was shrinking fast. He watched the girl's chest. It continued to rise and fall.

Cincinnati read aloud. "It is the duty of the field agent to rebuild in the event of a total collapse. The agent must attempt to commandeer local radio facilities. If none are available, the agent must use the following guide to construct a transmitter and tower using any obtainable conductive material."

The DJ sat across the kitchen table from the girl with the orange bucket, staring into her eyes. "Conductive material?" he asked.

Cincinnati ran her fingers through the girl's hair and smiled. "She's a beautiful little antenna."

•

Memphis kicked in the door of his next-door neighbors' house. He had introduced himself when they'd first moved in, but he couldn't remember their names. They were a middle-aged couple with two young boys that they home-schooled. The boys had long hair and played baseball in the yard at odd hours. Whenever Memphis made eye contact with the boys they would look shyly away and go back to their pitching drills.

The inside of the house was clean and orderly. Memphis led Cincinnati through the empty living room and into the kitchen. Next to the sink, dishes were laid on a towel to dry, the utensils lined up by type, the forks with the forks and the spoons with the spoons. Memphis turned on his flashlight and made his way down the hallway toward the bedrooms. The first room he opened belonged to one of the boys. Life-sized posters of baseball players covered the walls. The next room was the parents' room. Small, hand-carved wooden boxes were lined up on their dresser.

Memphis found the family in the last room of the house. It was set up as a classroom. The boys were at their school desks and the mother sat at a large oak desk. The father stood looking out the window. The kids' books were open to pictures of dinosaurs.

Memphis stood in the doorway for a moment without speaking. "Sorry to bother you. We knocked and no one answered."

"They're affected," Cincinnati said. "I don't think they can hear you."

In the light from the window Memphis could see dust particles floating through the still air.

Cincinnati took the father by the hand and turned him to face her. "Roughly 220 pounds," she said. "Muscular. Should be able to project a good signal." She grabbed the mother's hand and led the couple out of the room.

"What about the boys?" Memphis called out to her.

"Bring them," Cincinnati said. "We'll keep the family unit together."

Memphis took the two boys' hands and followed Cincinnati. "We're not going far," he told them, but they didn't protest. Their feet shuffled as they followed alongside Memphis. Their hair hung in their eyes.

Cincinnati led them to the center of the cul-de-sac at the end of the street. She made a circle of the family, clasping their hands together, positioning them with their heads up and their mouths open. Memphis caught her eye as she stuck her fingers in the youngest boy's mouth to pull his jaw open. "Increases the signal capacity," she said. "The head is full of fluids." She stepped back to admire her work. "All right," she said. "Now let's get the rest of them."

They went through every house on the street, gathering the residents and placing them in a cluster in center of the cul-de-sac. "Make sure they're touching," Cincinnati said. "The connection has to be solid."

In a small yellow house with one bedroom, Memphis found pictures of the girl with the orange bucket. A woman sat in the front room, in a chair by the TV. When he put the woman in the cluster, he went back to his own house and led the girl with the orange bucket from the dining table. "Your mom is looking for you," he told the girl. He placed her small hand in her mother's hand and pressed them tight. The circle was growing quickly. The affected didn't try to sit down or shield their eyes from the sun. Looking up with their mouths open, they seemed to be frozen in the middle of a collective scream.

By the end of the day Memphis' feet were sore. He had bruised his heel kicking open locked doors. Standing next to the cluster of bodies, he watched their chests rise and fall in unison. He squinted, sure that it was an illusion. Cincinnati stood next to him with her clipboard at her side. "What's wrong?" she asked.

"Their breathing," Memphis said. "Listen."

Memphis held his breath to hear more clearly. Every person in the cul-de-sac was inhaling and exhaling at the same time. If Memphis closed his eyes, the breathing sounded like bicycle tires on a gravel road.

5

At the table, the cereal bowl was still untouched, the milk curdled and stinking. Cincinnati sat in the middle of the living room surrounded by a tangle of copper wires threaded between random hunks of electronic equipment. Memphis wanted to ask her what each piece was for, but didn't want to interrupt. Cincinnati's hands moved quickly in the dim light. The house was lit only by candles, which made the wires appear to glow. She turned screwdrivers and pinched wire cutters, paused to read from a thick black binder, then looked back down at her work. Memphis paced in the kitchen. Beetles and moths threw themselves against the windows, trying to get at the candlelight. Their wings vibrated against the glass. Memphis walked to the window and cupped his hands to block out the reflection of the candles. There was no moon. The street was so dark he couldn't see the house next door.

Binders lay open on the floor, surrounding Cincinnati. She flipped through schematics and specifications, running her finger along tables and charts, then looking back at the wires. Dissected DVD players and car stereos splayed out in front of her. She placed alligator clips on a bare metal terminal and the devices around her began to whir, fans spinning, orange and green lights appearing on all the different parts. Memphis watched in amazement, careful not to block the light from the candles.

The DJ had raided the liquor cabinets in Memphis' neighbors' houses. He sat on the back patio, drinking and singing in the dark. "I've got the Adderall blues, there's holes in my shoes," he slurred, holding a marker to his face as though it were a microphone. "This next track goes out to the mosquitoes and the palmetto bugs. Some call them pests, but you and I understand they're just trying to play their role in all this chaos, keep us skating on the edge of this collapse, eat the blood we don't need and the food we don't finish, the things we leave behind without thinking, because that's what we do, isn't it? Leave things behind without thinking? Isn't that just a hallmark of humanity? Call in now with your thoughts."

The large clock on the living room wall continued to tick. Memphis wondered how long its batteries would hold out. He eyed the second hand carefully. It seemed to be moving slower already. He counted, "One Mississippi, two Mississippi," but his rhythm was out of sync with the clock and he couldn't tell which one was right. He sat in the recliner and watched the hands move around in circles until he fell asleep.

•

The transmitter stood as a proper object in the middle of Memphis' living room, black and silver guts exposed. Memphis followed a trail of jumper cables outside, where he found Cincinnati in a driveway three houses down, connecting her homemade transmitter to a neighbor's truck.

"How far can the signal reach?" Memphis asked.

"Depends on the height," Cincinnati said.

She continued splicing jumper cables and making her way down the street. Memphis followed close behind, straightening the cables when they twisted up. They moved from house to house and eventually toward the cul-de-sac. The group of affected was exactly as they had been the day before. Their open jaws made them appear bored. Memphis looked from face to face, trying to remember who lived where, which ones he had seen at the neighborhood park, which ones he had seen at the grocery store, but they were indistinguishable. He had seen names inside their houses—on business cards, calendars, monogrammed shirt collars, name tags—but now he couldn't recall any of them. When he tried, the syllables sounded off. Things he knew to be names seemed inappropriate now.

Cincinnati stood silently behind the girl with the orange bucket, holding a pair of alligator clips at her sides. "This might hurt," she whispered to the girl, then opened the clips and clamped them on the girl's wrists. The affected all inhaled simultaneously. Their eyes fluttered.

"You're on," Cincinnati yelled at the DJ, who, still drunk, leaned in the doorway of Memphis' house. He held a cheap microphone up to his mouth and began to talk.

"Here we are at the end of days, the time after the time after, like the silent part of the night when you wake up and regret all of the things you've said and done and been. All of the songs we thought were leading us up to this moment were sad imitations of how desperate it feels. I remember sitting in a tree as a kid, listening to the sounds of car stereos going by on the highway, thinking, if I could just get inside one of those cars, get out of my parents' yard, that everything would be better, that the welts from mosquito bites and fire ant bites would itch less, that my skin condition would heal, that I'd be able to swim like the other kids down at the spring, that my voice would stop cracking and settle into a more refined register like the men I heard on the radio at night, after my family had fallen asleep, when I lay in bed with the covers over my head, listening at the lowest possible volume."

Cincinnati moved between the cars, turning the keys in the ignition of each one until the engines were humming together, sending power to the transmitter, sending radio waves through the affected. She turned the car radios to the same emergency frequency and the DJ's voice poured out of the open car windows and echoed against the walls of the houses. The affected twitched with small muscle spasms, the radio waves moving through them, their heads tilting farther back, their jaws opening wider and wider as though they were trying to swallow the sky.

•

Cincinnati sat in the back of the FCC van while Memphis drove slowly through quiet intersections, down streets filled with unmoving cars. The affected were everywhere: a group of children jumping rope, arms at their sides, the rope slack on the ground between them; a man next to an open car door, a suitcase at his feet; a teenager lying on the ground beneath a bicycle—the condition, it seemed, had affected him in the middle of pedaling. Civilization had only been in collapse for a few days, but the grass was already tall and unruly. It rose up next to the sidewalk, hiding the feet and shins of the affected.

"The signal's getting weaker," Cincinnati said, twisting knobs and flipping switches, measuring the broadcast capacity of the collection of bodies. "Slow down."

Memphis slowed the van to an idle. On the radio, the DJ discussed songs he had no way of playing. "I remember the song that was on the radio the night I lost my, dare I say it, virginity. It was about being stuck in a motel room in a city far from home, waiting for someone to call, but, as we know, no one will ever call again, our telecommunications infrastructure was fragile, more fragile than we could ever have imagined, just a thin web between us, the massive cables laid beneath the ocean and buried in the ground under our homes just physical manifestations of our ultimate isolation."

As the van moved away from Memphis' house, the static rose from the background of the transmission until Memphis had to strain to make out the words. He could only decipher pieces of the DJ's sentences. "… arrested for noncompliance… any unfinished business… blues and bluegrass and jazz…" Then it cut out altogether.

"Stop," Cincinnati said. They were less than a mile from Memphis' front door. "Here's where the signal ends."

Memphis put the van in park. The needles on Cincinnati's equipment all lay flat. He looked out the window as though seeing his neighborhood for the first time, the absence of movement allowing him to appreciate the way the light hit safety reflectors in the street, the way the pavement cracked near the bases of tall oak trees.

"What's that?" Cincinnati asked, pointing at a sign through the windshield. Memphis had seen it so many times he hadn't even noticed it had changed. At the top of the sign, white letters on a burgundy background: First Elemental

Church of Christ the Soft-Spoken. Beneath it, marquee letters ordinarily reserved for the week's sermon spelled out:

WE ARE THE UNTOUCHED EARDRUM

INQUIRE WITHIN

Cincinnati and Memphis pushed open the large wooden door of the church. The room was dark, illuminated only by the sunlight filtering through tall stained-glass windows. The windows depicted scenes of men in white robes covering their ears, wrapping bandages around their heads, lying on the ground, bleeding, red glass leaking from their ears. The pews were full of worshipers, though none of them moved. Some held their hands above their heads in praise, some held their hands clasped together in front of their lips. Memphis tried to find the pastor's followers from the radio station, but they all looked too similar. At the front of the room, on a small stage, the pastor sat with his hands in his lap, his head lowered, his eyes closed.

"Welcome," he said without opening his eyes. "Please help yourself to the coffee and doughnuts."

Cincinnati stormed up the center aisle between the pews, holding her clipboard out in front of her. "I've got a list of infractions here." She tore off a pink piece of paper and waved it around.

The pastor slowly opened his eyes, blinked, then took the paper from Cincinnati. "Destruction of broadcast infra-structure during a time of national crisis? Obstruction of a FCC field agent?" He dropped the slip of paper, letting it float to the ground. "This space is a sanctuary," he said.

Memphis stood at the back of the room. The silhouettes of

the congregation blended together in the dim light. He tried to think of them as separate entities, each with a family, a job, a hobby, a nightly oral hygiene routine, but he couldn't picture them at home, alone. They fit perfectly together in this place. Memphis held his hands together in front of his mouth and looked down at the floor, mimicking the congregation. He expected to feel peaceful, but instead he felt strained, trying to make out the patterns on the floor in the dim light.

"The arm of the FCC is flexible and wide," Cincinnati said. "I have the authority to enter any structure I deem to be a threat to our national communications network."

The pastor leaned forward with his elbows on his knees. "You're always welcome here," he said. "We can make room for more." He waved his hand at the congregation and they began to shift in the darkness. Memphis couldn't tell which ones were moving and which ones remained still. They shuffled their feet quietly on the floor but their hands stayed in place. Their heads didn't move. After a moment, Memphis could see that there was an empty space in the middle of one of the aisles, just large enough for two people. The pastor lowered his head. "You may take your places."

Cincinnati picked up the piece of paper from the floor and stuck it to the top of her clipboard. Memphis backed up a few steps. The room seemed smaller than when they first entered, the windows darker, the ceiling lower, the large cross at the back of the stage, behind the pastor, tilting forward toward him. He couldn't tell if it had been that way all along or if it was in the process of slowly falling. He continued backing up, watching for any additional movement in the crowd, watching Cincinnati make notes on her clipboard, until he bumped into something. He thought it was the large wooden door, but when he reached behind him his hand found something soft.

"Stay," a woman's voice whispered into his ear. "We have coffee and doughnuts for everyone."

Memphis turned to face the voice. The woman wore a faded blue dress. She nodded toward a table at the back of the room covered in half-eaten doughnuts and spilled coffee. She held out two white foam cups. "It's not hot, but it's strong." Memphis brushed past her, opened the heavy wooden door, and walked out toward the van.

6

I t was Memphis' idea to stack them. The affected were compressed into the cul-de-sac, leaning into each other, hands intertwined, chins pressed against backs of heads. They were becoming a solid object. Memphis circled the group, pressing on shoulders, testing the strength of the formation. "I think they can bear the load," he told Cincinnati. She thumbed through a large black binder.

"The higher we can go, the longer our range will be," Cincinnati said.

They expanded their search for the affected, spreading out to the surrounding streets and neighborhoods. Memphis found a family of three huddled under a blanket in the living room of a small house in a gated community. The boy was only three or four. Memphis guided the parents to a standing position, then placed the boy in the mother's arms, lacing her fingers behind his back and positioning him on the mother's hip in the same way Memphis had seen so many mothers carry their children through grocery stores and parks. He held the woman's hands as they held the child, expecting her arms to drop to her sides under the weight, but when Memphis let go the woman's arms tightened. The veins in her forearms stood out. She held fast. Memphis looped the husband's arm through the crook of her elbow and led the family a half-mile to the cul-de-sac, where Cincinnati waited beside a stepladder.

Memphis guided the family up the three steps. Taking the husband by the arm, he led them slowly across the pile, pausing frequently to test the strength of the bodies, poking forward with his toe before placing all of his weight. The pile held firm. The affected made small grunts and exhalations as Memphis stepped on their shoulders and heads. He placed the young mother at the center of the pile, then placed her husband in front of her, cradling the man's arms around mother and child.

The work went fast. By the end of the day, Memphis and Cincinnati had cleared an entire neighborhood, leaving behind front doors splintered at the deadbolts. The DJ followed behind, packing cans of food and bottles of liquor into a shopping cart.

Later they sat on Memphis' front porch, each with a glass of whiskey, watching the sun go down behind the pile of bodies that by this point had grown two tiers higher. Memphis looked at his hands. He had led the affected all day through side streets and tall grass, holding their elbows and forearms, sometimes their shirtsleeves and collars, and the work had blistered his skin. He flexed his hands closed and then open again, the skin cracking and splitting open. He touched the sore at the corner of his mouth and, although he could feel the roughness in the way it vibrated under his finger, he could not feel anything at all in his fingertip. The skin felt like someone else's.

They stacked for days, until the pile of bodies became a tower. The bodies were stacked so high they blocked out the afternoon sun.

Wires ran back and forth across the street. Cincinnati had gathered cars from surrounding intersections, linking them to each other and her transmitter to improve the signal quality. She would clear a jammed intersection of both its cars and its affected, filling the driveways and curbs of Memphis' street, while Memphis escorted new bodies to the tower. The bodies grew narrower and narrower until they came to a point with a single young woman in a thin brown dress, whom Memphis had dragged to the top of the steep slope.

"Let's get wacky," the DJ said into the microphone, sober for the first time in days. He had rigged up a record player and a stack of looted records. "It might be the end of days, but it's the beginning of our new lives. What are the odds of anyone out there hearing this? We've got a representative from the United States government and she assures me that there is a plan in place involving helicopters, flags, other symbols that we've come to rely on—things painted neatly on the sides of vehicles, letters, abbreviations, forms with spaces too small for the information they require, photocopies that lose clarity with each successive generation, lines that stretch around large gray buildings, shoe repair, the way your voice sounds when you have a sinus infection, the comparative distances between your feet and your shoulders. It's the soundtrack for the end of the world or the beginning of the world, depending on how you look at it, and it all starts now." The DJ lifted the needle and placed it on top of a spinning record.

Memphis stood in the front doorway as the music reverberated down his street from the open car windows. The cars idled, their headlights off. The smell of exhaust was comforting. Something unseen was functioning as expected. In the living room, Cincinnati moved between equipment, taking notes and hurrying from one piece of machinery to the next. The sun was setting behind the tower of bodies. Around the jagged silhouette of arms and legs and heads, the sky turned pink at the horizon, fading up to dark blue above them. Memphis hadn't even noticed the weather changing, but now he could feel fall coming. The sky was clear. In the absence of artificial light it looked deeper. Memphis choked back the feeling that if he stared upward for long enough he might fall into it. He closed his eyes, dizzy.

Near the end of the song, Cincinnati handed the DJ a piece of paper. The DJ let the last notes of the song linger before picking up the microphone. "I've just been handed a message. All survivors should come to our broadcast location, address to follow. Bring any loved ones affected by the epidemic, including family members and small pets, any and all prescription medications, and appropriate documentation of your illnesses, deformities, and desires."

That night, Memphis and Cincinnati fell asleep in Memphis' twin bed, their arms touching. The DJ's voice vibrated through the bedroom door, the bass lines of the music gently rattling the window in its frame.

·

In the morning, Memphis walked around the base of the tower. The grass at the edges of the street was wet with dew.

He put his blistered hands on the backs and shoulders of the affected and occasionally recoiled in pain as pieces of dry skin at the edges of his blisters caught on fabric and loose threads. The flesh was so dense he could only see a few inches into the pile. Remembering news stories about people being trampled to death at rush hour on subway platforms, Memphis worried about the girl with the orange bucket and her mother being at the center of the pile, but the way the bodies continued to move slightly, in synchronicity, with inhalations and exhalations, gave him faith. None of them had eaten in how long? A week? Two? He had already lost track. Suddenly, he realized he might never again know the date.

Through the broken skin on his hands, Memphis thought he felt a vibration. He pressed his ear between the shoulder blades of a large man, taller than Memphis by six or eight inches, and listened. He could hear the man's heartbeat, though it seemed quieter than it should have been. Pressing the side of his face harder against the man's back, his cheek flattening against the man's spine, Memphis found what he was looking for. The vibration was there, somewhere in the layers of muscle and fat. He felt it in his jawbone.

•

"How long can someone go without eating?" Memphis asked Cincinnati as she tinkered with the transmitter in the living room.

"These are exceptional circumstances," she said. "Things that used to make sense don't make sense anymore."

"The tower seems steady," Memphis said, "but I don't know how long they can hold out." He touched the scab at the corner of his mouth, then the welt in the crook of his elbow.

"What's the weight limit of the human skeleton?"

Cincinnati crossed the room and stood in front of Memphis. She took his hands in hers, touching the blisters gently, feeling their outlines with the tips of her fingers, looking intently at them as though they might open up and puddle out onto the blue-gray carpet. "I felt something this morning," she said, putting his hand on her stomach. "It's growing."

Memphis spread his fingers, trying to cover as much of her surface area as he could. Here, too, was the vibration. He wondered if it was coming from the radio waves or from his own bones.

•

The first survivors showed up with cars packed full of suitcases and canned goods. Cincinnati directed them to an empty house and took down their medical histories. "There are bylaws," she said, flipping through a swollen binder. "No unscheduled events. No self-deprecating humor. Follow the permit application process for such family traditions as birthday parties and bridal showers."

One of the first arrivals was a woman in a dark brown pickup truck. A black and white dog sat in the middle of the bench seat, and in the passenger seat, her adult son sat with his eyes wide and his mouth slightly open. "He just set the university's record for long jump," she said.

Memphis nodded and held eye contact while he listened.

"His roommate called and said he'd been acting funny, so I went to pick him up. Hasn't said the first thing since I got him. Won't eat a bite."

Cincinnati made notes on her clipboard. "We're still

working out how to best care for the affected," she said.

Memphis opened the boy's door and helped him out of the car.

The mother looked up at the stack of bodies. "Please don't put him in there."

"Your son will be part of the solution," Memphis said.

The woman wept into the sleeve of her shirt.

Cincinnati leaned into the car window. "Let me show you to your house," she said. "We have an airy one-bedroom with a beautiful flower garden just down the block."

•

Within two weeks, dozens of survivors had repopulated Memphis' neighborhood. They grilled canned ham over open fires on the pavement. Children laughed in the street, running circles around the base of the tower, grabbing onto the legs of the affected and peering around, taking cover behind the bodies during games of hide and seek. Life started to feel normal. The DJ stayed in the living room, broadcasting twelve hours a day and sleeping the other twelve. The survivors brought him records, and he dedicated songs to the people outside.

A doctor arrived, still wearing a white lab coat stained gray with sweat. She set up shop in the yard of a small house that Cincinnati picked out. A line of people with deep coughs and ingrown toenails formed at her door. She laid them on a wooden picnic table and performed delicate operations using only a pocketknife and a glass thermometer.

Soon after the doctor arrived, Memphis sat across the picnic table from her. He held out his hands, palms upward.

"You really opened yourself up," the doctor said.

Memphis studied the woman's face. "How old are you?" he asked the doctor.

"Bend your fingers," the doctor said.

Memphis tried to curl his fingers inward but the blistered skin and dried pus stopped him. The doctor took out a towel and wet it with a bottle of water. She wiped down Memphis' hands, scrubbing away the pus and blood that had gathered in the creases of his knuckles. Memphis tried again to flex his fingers, but this time the pain stopped him.

"How long has it been since you've had full use of your hands?"

Memphis thought. Time had taken on the qualities of a long-distance relationship. He remembered what it looked like but couldn't remember how it felt. His hands were cratered with burst-open blisters. He didn't know how to answer her.

The doctor shook her head. "This is the best I can do," she said, covering Memphis' hands with a thick ointment and wrapping them in bandages. "You'll need to change these daily. It's important to keep the wounds clean."

Memphis found Cincinnati at the end of the street, giving directions to a group of survivors on the care and maintenance of the affected in the tower. "Listen to their breathing," she said. "Take measurements of their chests and biceps every six hours. Watch for signs of deterioration."

Memphis looked down at his bandaged hands. They had lost their definition. Their shapes were blunted, the fingers wrapped together. He held them up to his nose. The smell of the antibiotic ointment hung in his nostrils.

When Cincinnati finished speaking, Memphis touched her on the shoulder. He could feel the pressure of her through the bandages. She looked at his hands for a long while before taking them in her own.

"Infection," he said.

Cincinnati sucked in a breath through her nose. "We have antibiotics. They found another pharmacy this morning." She traced the cloth bandages with her fingers. "You need rest," she said, gently pulling him toward the house.

The bedroom stank of old sweat. Cincinnati opened the window, but no breeze came through to clear the stale air. She laid Memphis down and rubbed between his eyes with her thumb. He put his bandaged hand on her stomach. "Can you still feel it?" he asked. It had only been a few weeks. The child inside her couldn't have been larger than a peach pit. She hadn't yet expanded to accommodate the extra life.

Cincinnati nodded. "It's a girl," she said.

Memphis held his bandaged hand against her but couldn't feel anything, not the movement of the child or the heat of Cincinnati's skin. He closed his eyes and tried to sense the rising and falling of her chest, but the cushion of the bandage prevented even that. His hands could only feel the deliberate squeeze of Cincinnati's fingers.

7

Memphis struggled with the feeling of being less useful than he had once been. When families arrived with more affected people who needed to be placed on the tower, his hands were too stiff to guide them into the right spots, so he tried to direct the healthy survivors from the ground. They rigged up a system of ropes and pulleys to lift the affected to the top of the tower, now two or three times taller than the highest oaks in the neighborhood. A former tree surgeon with a gnarled thumb led the effort to raise the affected into the places Memphis pointed out.

"A little bit to the right," Memphis yelled from the base of the tower, trying to cup his hands around his mouth to project his voice. It didn't work. The bandages absorbed the sound.

The tree surgeon clasped an affected man's shirt with four fingers, his thumb sticking straight up, refusing to bend. The tree surgeon guided the affected man into a gap in the tower and disconnected the pulley from the man's belt buckle, then climbed down and stood next to Memphis.

"How's that, boss?"

Memphis put his bandaged hand on his chin and nodded. It wasn't where he would have placed the body, but he didn't say anything.

"One thing I learned from the tree business," the tree surgeon said, back on the ground, "is you never know what something looks like from street level."

Memphis stared at the man's deformed thumb. It had been nearly severed in a chainsaw accident and only resembled a thumb in its outline. It had no nail and no knuckle. The doctors had taken skin from other places on his body to shape it around the splintered bone.

"You're up there, and everything is moving, and you can see so far, it's easy to lose perspective. Things look all different."

"Sure," Memphis said. "That sounds about right."

•

Memphis held a can of ravioli between his bandaged hands. He could see the can slipping out of his grip and tried to tighten his fingers around it, but the can fell to the linoleum and left a dent in the dirty, off-white floor. Cincinnati picked the can up and opened it for him. "So much sodium," she said, reading the label before dumping the can into a bowl.

Memphis sat down at the table and pinched a fork between his bandaged hands, then tried to stab it into the bowl of pasta. The fork slipped out of his grip and fell onto the floor. Without speaking, Cincinnati picked up the fork and began putting bites into Memphis' mouth. As he chewed, she read from her clipboard, flipping pages with her right hand, scooping up pieces of ravioli with her left. Memphis looked at the side of her face. Her eyes moved down the page, jumping from word to word without pausing. Her pupils expanded and contracted. The ravioli was cold and the sauce was thick. After eating half of the bowl, he waved his hand to tell Cincinnati he was done. She shrugged and ate the rest, putting huge forkfuls of food in her mouth with each bite before heading outside. Memphis watched from the window as she gathered the survivors together at the base of the tower.

"We have to increase our broadcast capacity," she said. "I am instituting a new Expanded Permissible Exposure Initiative. The regulations regarding how close people were supposed to be to sources of radio frequencies are remnants of the past. We have to move forward without fear." She asked if anyone felt ill or had developed double vision. No one raised a hand.

As the survivors stood around Cincinnati in a circle, Memphis saw a pack of dogs between homes across the street. He'd seen them a few times before, hovering at the edge of the neighborhood where the road turned to dirt. The dogs seemed sleepy and subdued until coming across some discarded cans of black beans and peaches on a picnic table in a neighbor's front yard. Two of the dogs hopped onto the bench, snapped the cans in their jaws, and hurried off toward the end of the street to lick the sharp metal clean.

Cincinnati adjourned the meeting and a young father chased his toddler around the neighborhood, reaching out to grab the back of her shirt whenever she tripped over a curb or a root. Memphis watched the two running in circles around the tower, the daughter smiling and laughing, then making their way toward the end of the street where the dogs lay underneath a dead grapefruit tree. The child squealed when she spotted the dogs, and the father was just able to snatch her up before she reached them. The dogs growled but didn't stand up. The young father backed away slowly. The dogs laid their heads on their paws. Memphis closed his eyes. It was hot. Nothing else moved.

•

As the sun set, a single trumpet blast rang out through the neighborhood.

"What's that noise?" one of the new arrivals asked.

"It's the church," Memphis said.

The trumpet rang for longer than usual. When it stopped, Memphis could see the pastor standing at the end of the street.

The pastor raised his hands into the air and closed his eyes. "Followers of the devil, riders of radio waves, chasers of disease and disappointment, look inside yourselves and find that you, too, believe this tower, this suspension of your loved ones, is an abomination under God, and truly you can be saved. We have heard the silence in the space between words, we have witnessed the power of the flat sound wave, we have speculated about the genetic makeup of deep-sea creatures with no need for hearing, how we might be made more like them, how their eyes and antennae can tell them more about the world than we could ever hope to know."

Memphis and Cincinnati followed the crowd gathering in front of the pastor, turning their backs to the tower as he spoke. "Look at your neighbors to the left and right of you," he said. "Look at their dirty faces and fingernails. Can't you sense their despair? We're at the brink of a great transformation. You there," he said, pointing to a teenage girl in a dirty gray dress. "You have family up in this tower, don't you?"

The girl nodded. "My mom and sister," she said.

The pastor shook his head and looked solemnly at her. The girl lowered her head as he put a hand on her shoulder. "These people took them from you? Put them in this pile?"

The girl nodded again, then sniffled, wiping her nose on the back of her hand.

"You won't be judged for this," the pastor said. He turned to address the crowd. "The ones who will stand judgment for this crime against the Lord, for this abrasion on the face of his perfect creation, will be the representatives of what remains of the United States government. What they couldn't accomplish with tax incentives and regulations they accomplished through the distortion of our greatest hopes and fears, our desire to connect with others of our kind, our fear that we may be living out our last moments on Earth in a kind of limbo, waiting for the blessed condition to overtake us, too. Tell me, girl, wouldn't you be happier to be back with your family, in your own house, situated comfortably in your living room, staring at each other, not moving? Don't you feel as though you've been forgotten here, alone, while your dear mother and sister have found peace?"

The girl nodded, still staring at the ground.

The pastor smiled and lifted the girl's chin to meet his eyes. "The Lord has not forgotten you, child. You are his treasured creation. The blessed condition will find each of us in time and then, when we look, unblinking, at the glory of his world, we will hear his voice for the first time. It will be so beautiful. It will be so beautiful." The pastor put his hand on the back of the girl's neck and turned one more time to face the crowd. "All are welcome at our congregation. We have coffee and doughnuts enough for everyone." He turned around and began leading the girl away from the tower.

Cincinnati stepped in front of the pastor and poked her finger into his chest. "These people gave their bodies so that we could bring more survivors here. There are lonely people out there, sitting across the table from their husbands and wives, watching them slowly waste away. We are learning to take care of them. We're rebuilding."

The pastor pushed Cincinnati's hand away and shook his head.

The girl walked with her head lowered to the end of the street, then stopped and turned to look back at the tower. The pastor leaned over and whispered something in her ear. The girl nodded and they turned the corner together, disappearing behind a tall hedge that had grown uneven, its crooked branches sticking out in all directions.

8

Cincinnati continued increasing the strength of the broadcast signal by wiring more cars to the power supply, running their engines on alternating schedules, letting them cool, then starting them back up again. The tree surgeon constructed scaffolding to help him move more bodies onto the tower. Memphis continued to help with the positioning, but he would get tired by the early afternoon and need to rest. The heat sat on top of everything. It rose in waves off the pavement, distorting the light, casting rippling shadows. The survivors had been trying to agree on what the date was, but none of them had been keeping accurate records. Even Cincinnati neglected to follow a calendar. Fall was so close to summer, but summer was always so long Memphis had no idea when it might end.

•

Memphis gestured with his bandaged hands to a gap where the tree surgeon might place a new arrival, an elderly man bent over at the ribs, his back stiff and slumped, in a yellow shirt with brown stitching.

"This one will fit perfect," the tree surgeon said.

The bandages stank of sweat and infection. They had run out of gauze, and Memphis hadn't changed them in days. As the sun rose his hands began to throb. The sweat on his forehead felt different, like it was leaking out of places it shouldn't have been. He left the rest of the day's work to the tree surgeon's discretion and got in line for the doctor.

The line stretched down the street. Some people waited in lawn chairs, others lay stretched out on the sidewalk. When Memphis reached the doctor, she told him not to worry about the smell. "Everything smells bad before it gets better," the doctor said without looking up. She held her stethoscope in the middle of his back.

"If everyone will fill out this intake paperwork, then this will all go much faster," the doctor said. She handed Memphis a clipboard to pass down the line. Handwritten questions lined the page: Do you feel like you might have a limb you've forgotten about? Do you sometimes head out at night intent on making bad decisions? Do you measure your height against those around you?

Memphis handed the clipboard to a woman behind him. She wore bright neon running gear, looked to be in her thirties, and had a goiter the size of a softball. "Do you have a pen?" she asked.

"No," Memphis said, and looked at the doctor.

"Someone stole mine," the doctor said. "They're always stealing pens."

Memphis walked down the line of patients, asking people if he could help. They were weak, sick, hungry, and few replied with more than a grunt. He was relieved. He wouldn't have known how to help even if they'd asked.

Cincinnati was undeniably pregnant, though the bump

at her midsection was still small. Memphis found her in the living room, adjusting dials on the transmitter and moving wires between machines. There wasn't much he could do with his hands wrapped up, but he held out his arms and carried her binders, holding them out for her when she needed to make a note or consult a reference guide.

"Is she moving?" Memphis asked as Cincinnati twisted a wrench in circles.

She stopped working. "I think so," she said. "It's hard to tell."

She had been sick in the mornings for a while, unable to eat anything before midday. Indoor plumbing was already a distant memory, and she had been throwing up out of Memphis' open bedroom window at sunrise.

"Do you think it's growing like a fungus, or more like a vine?" Memphis asked.

Cincinnati started turning the wrench again. "It's too hard to explain," she said. "It's like the way the tide doesn't seem to be rising, but then all of a sudden your feet are wet."

•

The community mostly settled into a routine after the first few months, or what felt like months at least, though there were still incidents. A mother would rush the tower, trying to reach her affected children, but the neighbors had learned how to restrain people without unnecessary force, holding them down without breaking bones or even major discomfort, sitting in the middles of the their backs until their breathing slowed, until they were able to regulate their emotions. They had developed an unofficial script:

"We've all lost people."

"My children are up there, too."

"I look for their silhouettes against the rising sun."

It was probably mid-to-late September, the community decided at one of Cincinnati's daily briefings. Neighbors stood among a mess of wires and jumper cables at the base of the tower.

"Can we agree that probably, based on the angle of the sun, it's not yet fall?" she asked the crowd gathered around her. The crowd nodded and looked down at the ground, unsure how to answer.

"It doesn't feel like my birthday yet," a middle-aged woman with graying red hair said. "My birthday always felt cold."

It wasn't cold, but Memphis could feel the air waiting to turn. He tried to remember when the first cold day of the year usually was. It seemed like maybe it was around Halloween. He remembered kids in their costumes at his door, shivering, their parents hovering behind them in the street, watching them closely, trying to resist the urge to stand beside them.

Memphis lost track of what people were saying. He looked toward the diseased grove at the end of the street. He remembered riding past acres and acres of orange groves, staring out the window of his parents' car, watching as the rows of trees lined up and split apart, like an optical illusion. The groves always seemed dead still and silent, like they were waiting for someone to deliver bad news.

•

The DJ sat in the living room of Memphis' house, his face unshaven, the hairs gray and black, the stink of whiskey hovering in the air around him. He held the microphone loosely in front of his face and spoke. "It's all emergency broadcasts all the time. We're perched on the collapsing front edge of humanity and the night is coming and we're unprepared. The FCC is here to help us, but what have they done for us lately? Come see for yourselves. We have a tower, we have broadcast power, we have a gathering place and a store of rations and little holes that we shit into on the edges of an orange grove and no one will ever eat those oranges again because they don't turn the colors they're supposed to turn and when you peel them open their flesh is dried out and stringy and tastes like poison and rot. I tried, I tried. This one goes out to the environmental scientists, the ones with big ideas about little ecosystems. We miss you and we're sorry. We'll leave the doors unlocked in case you come back."

·

Cincinnati wasn't the only pregnant one among the survivors. A young woman had shown up by herself, on foot. She brushed stray hairs out of her face as Memphis and Cincinnati showed her to a small one-bedroom bungalow at the end of the street, in the cul-de-sac directly facing the tower. "There's just enough room here for you to grow into," Cincinnati said to the young woman. "Did you leave many people behind?"

The pregnant woman nodded.

"The father?" Cincinnati asked.

The pregnant woman looked up at the tower.

"There are so many up there," Cincinnati said. "I've got the total number somewhere." Memphis held a binder on top of his outstretched arms and Cincinnati took it from him, flipping to a page in the middle. "Three hundred and thirty-seven," she said. "Hard to believe, isn't it? We started with just a collection of neighbors. As a matter of fact, the woman who lived in your house is almost at the center of the bottom layer. She lived there by herself. Not like you. Do you mind?" Cincinnati reached out toward the pregnant woman's belly, but the woman turned away. "I'm sorry," Cincinnati said. "How far along are you?"

The woman held her hands across the bottom of her swollen belly and looked down at the bulge of her belly button poking out under the fabric of her shirt. "I lost track," she said.

"It's okay," Cincinnati said. "It's normal to lose count. We have a doctor here."

"I don't trust doctors," the woman said. She went into the house and closed the door, then peeked out through the curtains. Cincinnati made a mark on her clipboard.

•

Memphis' bandaged hands stank more every day. He reached up to scratch the scab in the corner of his mouth and the cotton bandage snagged the jagged edge. He pulled and the scab came off, the sore leaking blood onto the yellowed bandage. He went to see the doctor.

"Let's have a little look," the doctor said, unwrapping Memphis' hands slowly, pulling back the bandages layer by layer and letting the long strips fall to the floor.

When the doctor was finished, Memphis could feel the sunlight on his hands. It was too hot. Hotter than it used to be. He closed his eyes and held his face up to the sky. The doctor leaned forward, cradling Memphis' hands gently in her own. "Wiggle your pinky fingers," the doctor said.

Memphis tried. He could feel the muscles in his forearm tense and release. He kept his eyes closed.

"Are you wiggling them?" the doctor asked.

Memphis didn't answer. He concentrated on the feeling of moving fingers, remembering the feeling of cold piano keys, the soft curves of Cincinnati's thighs. He remembered picking his nose and picking scabs and scratching mosquito bites. When he opened his eyes, the doctor was staring at him.

"They're not moving," she said.

Memphis looked down at his shriveled hands. The blisters had healed, but in their place black circles covered the surface of his palms. Thin black lines extended from the circles, snaking out over the arteries on his wrists and fading as they climbed higher up his forearms, up toward, Memphis knew, his heart.

9

Memphis tried to sleep but his hands felt like someone else's hands. When he woke up in the middle of the night, needing to piss, he raised his arms in the air above his head. His hands flopped downward, lifeless. He tried to make fists but nothing moved. In the moonlight coming through his bedroom window, his hands looked unfamiliar. They were the wrong sizes. The fingernails were too long. The knuckles were too skinny. He imagined holding Cincinnati's hands, running his fingers through her hair, but couldn't quite remember the sensations. All he could feel was a warm ache. He reached across the bed to Cincinnati, extending his arms until he felt the resistance of her skin, but he couldn't feel anything with any precision. He could feel the blunt shape of her, the mass of an object in his bed, an indistinct form underneath the blanket, but not her vertebrae, not her ribs, not her collarbone. He pressed his face into the pillow. The sun began to rise.

When Cincinnati woke up, Memphis had already been awake for what felt like hours. His dying hands rested on his chest. Cincinnati rolled over in bed and ran her fingers from his elbow to the tips of his fingers. "I think she'll have your hands," she said.

Memphis held his breath for a second.

In the morning light, the shadows from the horizontal blinds fell across Cincinnati's face, making her look camouflaged. Memphis' eyes traced the way the shadows bridged her nose and her cheeks. "How do you know?" he asked.

"I can just tell," she said. "Weather patterns. Something in my throat."

Memphis swallowed and he could feel it, too, at the bottom of his throat. Something. He closed his eyes and inhaled. It smelled like fall.

•

A red-haired boy stood near the end of the street, throwing rocks at the pack of dogs and laughing. With each rock, the dogs scattered, then regrouped. They eyed the boy carefully, staying far enough away that the rocks bounced off the pavement in front of them.

"They're just hungry," Memphis said. "We should be trying to help them."

"They're sick," the red-haired boy said. "My dad says they're mean. He says we can't have dog friends anymore. There's no such thing as a pet. Have you smelled their breath?"

Memphis shook his head. A gray dog stepped away from the pack and moved toward them, growling.

"Look," the red-haired boy said. "They're not even tame. They think people are just something to bite." He threw a rock and hit the dog in the side. It backed away but kept its eyes on the boy. The boy picked up a basketball and walked back toward the cul-de-sac. There was a hoop in front of a driveway and the boy took shot after shot as Memphis watched until the ball bounced off the rim and into the bushes. "Just a little short," the boy said. "Just a little short."

•

By now the survivors expected the trumpet blast at sunset, but it still unnerved them. They looked in the direction of the sound, wrinkling their foreheads and squinting their eyes to see against the light from the setting sun. Memphis scanned the crowd. The faces were starting to look familiar. He recognized them by their answers on the forms Cincinnati handed out. Their family histories were sad and confusing. The people they loved had died or abused them. Memphis felt filled up by their sadness, but they seemed to bear it without noticing.

As the survivors went back to eating and talking around small campfires, Memphis noticed the prayer group from the pastor's church gathered at the end of the street. They stood in a circle, holding hands, heads lowered. Memphis approached them, his dead hands dangling at his sides. He could see that their mouths were moving. "We have food," he said, but no one answered him. As he got closer, he could hear them whispering a prayer.

"God, bless our neighbor. If we pray for rain, let it flood his fields. Let the rivers run over his banks. Let the current sweep our neighbor to the sea, where our savior lives in and among the marine life, in holy symbiosis. Forgive our neighbor for his selfish desire to rattle your precious air with his voice box, using it to make lists and demands. Willful ignorance is no excuse, Lord, and we know this. Make this clear to our neighbor, the false shepherd, who is leading your disciples away from green pastures. Use us as your instruments. Work through our hands and fingernails. Grow out of our skin like stiff hairs. Grow inward where we try to resist you, Lord, raising bumps and filling us with pus where we fall short of your plans for us. These things we pray in your name. Amen."

Memphis looked at each member of the prayer circle, one by one, but they never met his eyes. He started to reach out, but he knew he wouldn't be able to feel them even if he touched them. He turned around. The survivors nearby were looking down at their feet, at the weeds growing up through cracks in the asphalt.

•

The next morning didn't feel any different. Memphis woke up next to Cincinnati, his hands numb, his eyes crusted over with sleep. The sunlight from the window still looked the same. The pictures on the walls of his bedroom were still slightly crooked. The whiskey smell of the DJ in the living room and the sounds of his voice still drifted beneath the door.

Memphis climbed out of bed, holding his limp hands against his chest, and wiggled the bedroom door open with his elbow. The DJ sat in the recliner and spoke sleepily into the microphone while a song played over the air. Memphis could only make out snippets of what the DJ was saying. "Echoes under the bridge from passing… never mind the element of surprise… open yourself to the corruption of the flesh." The DJ's eyes were half-closed. His hair had fallen into his face. He set the needle down on a wobbly record, and the song that followed was so out of place that Memphis feared the man had lost his touch.

The house was dirty. Somewhere along the way they had stopped cleaning the carpet. Memphis looked around the room. Dirty footprints led from the kitchen to the living room and bedroom. Dead oak leaves were piled in a corner. Empty cans of ravioli and mixed vegetables were stacked on the counter. Cincinnati's binders lay spread out on the dining table, their photocopied pages scribbled over with blue and black ink, wrinkled with humidity.

Outside, grasshoppers thumped against the windows. Memphis pictured them swarming over the trees and bushes in the yard, their black bodies lined with yellow stripes, their tiny legs covered with spines. Later it would be the frogs. They had gotten louder. At dusk they made so much noise Memphis had a hard time focusing on anything else. He stood for a moment in the middle of the room. Life had changed so dramatically that he couldn't point to the exact moment he'd become accustomed to the way it was now.

When the screaming started in the street, Memphis first thought it was a low-flying airplane. The sound built and Memphis rubbed the backs of his limp hands against his eyes. The room came more clearly into focus. Memphis ran to the front door and jammed his elbow against the round knob. It twisted partially and then slipped against his skin. He pressed down on it again and again, rotating it almost open before he lost traction. After several attempts he got it unlatched and pulled the door open.

A group of women stood in a circle in front of his house. Memphis pushed his way through to the center of the group. The red-haired boy stood there, the basketball between his feet, staring straight ahead. A woman knelt in front of him, holding one of his hands between her own.

"Please," she said, "answer me. Please answer me."

The boy's jaw clenched, but he didn't speak. The woman opened her mouth and the sound she made echoed off the fronts of the houses, rose over the sound of the car engines powering the transmitter. It came back to Memphis, it seemed, from every direction. The other women in the circle looked at each other.

Above the screaming and shuffling sounds of the women, a voice boomed down the street. "Praise the Lord," the pastor said, smiling as he took long strides toward the circle of people. "Praise the Lord." He smiled and held his hands straight out at his sides. "We have prayed for this day and now it is here. This young child, this lover of nature and the green earth, has been called home. Are you his mother?" he asked, kneeling down and placing his hand on the woman's back. She nodded and sobbed into her folded hands. "What an honor," he said. "You've delivered another soul into the great restful silence, the ocean between this world and the next. Look into your son's eyes," he said, lifting her chin upward. "Does this look like the boy you raised? Like the boy that was once a part of you?"

The woman caught her sobs and looked intently at her son. "When he was little I caught him tearing the tails off lizards," she said. "He told me they would grow back even better. He was so happy."

"And now?" the pastor asked.

"I can't tell if he's still in there," she said. "He's wiggling a little bit."

"Just like a lizard's tail," the pastor said. The woman nodded and started sobbing again. "These are the twitches of muscles that have seen the rise and fall of heaven. Atrocities like this," he gestured toward the tower, "claim to raise up humanity, but the Lord has made us from the dust. We must look downward and inward if we want to find his everlasting love."

"This grief is not your engine," Cincinnati said. She stood in the doorway of Memphis' house, holding a binder open in her left hand, pointing directly at the pastor with her right. "According to section 113.5 A of the FCC Emergency Field Operations Manual, you are currently engaged in the manipulation of a survivor's emotional tragedy without regard for their overall well-being. This is punishable by a fine not to exceed five hundred dollars and up to six months in jail."

The pastor smiled and took the grieving woman's hand. "The silence draws closer with each muffled breath." The woman took her son's hand and followed the pastor away from the tower, to the end of the street. They walked slowly, the boy's shoes scraping against the sidewalk, his eyes shifting from side to side. After they rounded the corner the woman let out one more scream, but it quickly faded, as though it had been smothered.

10

Cincinnati had binders full of statistics about the survivors, had studied their average ages and the frequency of different medical conditions and food allergies. She had charted their family trees, including the affected relatives they placed in the tower. She had diagrammed the likelihood of certain recessive genes to appear in the group's potential offspring: blue eyes, red hair, harelips, drooping eyelids. She had gathered them together. Memphis had led them to food supplies. The tree surgeon had stacked their loved ones in a useful formation. The doctor had treated minor infections and ordinary signs of aging. Their needs were met. But what was it all for? The question rippled through the survivors.

One morning, the woman in the wheelchair waited outside the door of Memphis' house. When Memphis and Cincinnati emerged, she was urging the chair forward then backward. Cincinnati stood in front of the woman with her binder open, pen hovering over the page, ready to take note of whatever the woman might say.

The woman was older than most of the survivors. She had shown up a few weeks before, and Cincinnati had placed her in a house with two other survivors who had arrived alone so that she would have help getting in and out of the chair. The woman looked up and down the street. No one else was outside yet. The grass next to the sidewalk was still wet with dew. "I know him," she said, almost whispering. "The pastor."

Cincinnati knelt down and started writing. "Go on," she said.

"He's a true believer," the woman said.

Memphis stood behind Cincinnati. He tried to clench his fists, but his fingers wouldn't move. He crossed his arms over his chest and tucked his black hands into his armpits.

"I'm ready to be unspooled," the woman said. She looked up at the tower. "My boy went on before me. He was a good kid. Got a mosquito bite, the next week he was in the hospital. The bus stopped coming. I can't go see him anymore."

"What hospital?" Cincinnati asked.

"I know he's not in there," the woman said. "Not really."

Across the street, the red-haired boy's basketball caught the breeze and began to roll toward the gutter. Memphis watched as it gathered speed, then came to rest against a storm drain, too big to roll any farther.

•

Memphis sat across the picnic table from the doctor, under a tarp hung for shade. She was running out of antibiotics, Memphis knew. He had seen Cincinnati's list of available supplies. There were more out there, somewhere, but the pharmacies in the suburbs had already been emptied and the ones closer to the city were so congested with vehicles and affected that search teams had a hard time reaching them. Supplies were starting to run low throughout the whole neighborhood. The survivors were still comfortable, but just beneath the surface Memphis could see their panic. The fear in them was like a caught snake. It twisted under the skin of their faces, in their temples and lips.

The doctor held Memphis' hands up to her nose and inhaled. "The smell is going away," she said. "That's not good." Memphis hadn't noticed. The doctor traced her finger over the black lines from Memphis' palm up to his wrist. They were a little bit longer than they had been the day before, Memphis thought, but he couldn't be sure. The change felt organic, destined to be. He had learned how to eat from a bowl by holding it in the crook of his elbow. He had learned to hug Cincinnati using only his biceps.

"I have to operate," the doctor said. She placed Memphis' hands on the table, palms upward, and flattened his fingers against the wood. She unrolled a towel beside his hands. Wrapped inside the towel were shiny medical tools. The tools looked to Memphis like scissors and knives.

"Are they clean?" he asked the doctor.

She stopped and held up a scalpel. In its tiny blade, Memphis could see reflections of the houses behind him, the people waiting in line to see the doctor, the tall grass growing over the edge of the sidewalk.

"See?" the doctor said. "Clean."

He looked at the tools again, then looked away, at the branches of the oak tree above him.

"Count the leaves," the doctor said.

Memphis felt pressure in his hands and inhaled deeply, but the pain he expected never came. He tried to distinguish the leaves from one another, but they were too far away and formed a brown-green mass, half-moon patterns from parasites and fungi blending their edges together.

"Close your eyes," the doctor said.

Memphis closed his eyes and watched patterns blotch his eyelids.

"Did you feel that?" the doctor asked.

Memphis shook his head.

"Keep your eyes closed."

Memphis could hear the grinding and feel the table shaking, but nothing else. He didn't try to move his hands. He heard the sounds of sawing, the sounds of bones breaking, a wet sound like a sloppy kiss. He shut his eyes tighter and felt the sweat collect on his forehead. He smelled burning hair, but still felt nothing. When he opened his eyes, the table was covered in blood and his hands lay flat like a pair of gloves. The doctor had cauterized the wound with a cast-iron pan that still smoked on the ground beside them.

"I had no choice," the doctor said.

"I know," Memphis said. "I know, I know, I know."

•

Memphis woke up on the couch in his living room in a fever, feeling disoriented and afraid. The DJ's voice droned from the recliner beside him, something about animals decomposing upstream, but the room sounded strangely muffled. Memphis rolled onto his side, blinking, trying to gather his thoughts. Cincinnati jumped up from the dining table and moved quickly to his side. She knelt by the couch and rubbed her thumb in the center of his forehead. "It's okay," she said. "It will be okay."

Memphis started to raise his hand to scratch at the scab in the corner of his mouth, but Cincinnati put her hand on his forearm and gently pressed it back down at his side. She opened a binder and began reading. "Maximum permissible exposure limits should be treated with caution. Take care to restrict the amount of time spent within range of a transmitter. There are no long-term studies on genetic abnormalities as a result of exceeding these exposure limits."

Memphis felt sleepy and restless. His legs scratched against the fabric of the couch. He looked at the windows, but the curtains were drawn shut. He suddenly wanted to know what time of day it was. He started to sit up. Cincinnati put her hand on the middle of his chest and leaned in close, brushed the hair off his forehead and kissed his cheek. "There's just as much of you as there ever was," she said. Memphis looked down at where his hands should have been, but instead there were just stumps bandaged in shredded T-shirts. Where the bandages ended the skin on his forearms was tender and pink.

Memphis moaned and fell back into the couch. He was dizzy. He breathed deeply through his nose, closed his eyes, and turned his head to the side, afraid he might vomit. When he opened his eyes, he saw a shoebox on the coffee table beside him, filled up with salt. The tips of his fingers poked out from the mounds of the white crystals. The fingernails were long and, on his fingertips, there on the table, far away from where they should have been, he could make out the concentric circles of his fingerprints, a pattern he'd never paid very close attention to, the ridges dancing and moving in the candlelight.

•

When Memphis gathered his strength, Cincinnati took him for a walk out of the neighborhood, holding him by the forearm as though he might fall. They sat in the diseased orange grove, the loose white sand beneath them shifting and filling in around their legs. "I want to preserve you," Cincinnati said. "I don't want you to rot."

Memphis scratched at his nose with the stump where his right hand used to be. It felt strange, this new distance from his forearm to his face. Not bad, just different. The pain was still intense. When he pressed the bandage against his nose he became suddenly aware of the area inside his wrist. He thought he could feel the bone there, against the skin of his face. It poked out through the bandage, hard, in the center of his stump.

"How long will she take to grow?" he asked.

Cincinnati looked up at the orange trees. "Weeks." she said. "Months. These branches have so many thorns."

It was true. Memphis remembered climbing orange trees when he was a child, reaching for the fruit always hanging, it seemed, just farther up than he could safely go. He'd come home at night with holes in his shirts and pants where the thorns had snagged the fabric, pulling threads loose, leaving spaces where the pale skin of his belly showed through. "I want them back," he said.

Cincinnati began to cry and put her head on Memphis' shoulder. "I want it all back," she said. "I want something to inspect." She grabbed one of Memphis' wrists with both hands and pulled his stump close to her face, pressing the stained bandage against her lips.

Memphis had always heard that amputees felt the sensation of having limbs where there were no limbs anymore, but he didn't feel that. Where his fingertips had been felt like a doorway. The space between his arms and the sky was shortened. Rain clouds gathered above them. Though they didn't know the exact date and probably never would again, this time of year the thunderstorms came regularly and hard, flooding the streets and backing up the storm drains. The rivers rose over their banks. Memphis was six during his first hurricane. He remembered his mother holding him in a closet as the portable radio gave updates. It was tornadoes, he remembered, that had caused much of the damage. They appeared on the front edge of the hurricane, their forward momentum swirling the air like bathwater, whipping through the tops of oak trees, splitting trunks down the middle, downing power lines, stripping bushes bare, leaving strands of Spanish moss layered across sidewalks and streets and driveways.

11

M emphis' hands cured on the coffee table in the living room, next to the couch where he and his fiancé had picked out colors for their wedding. She had brought home stacks of wedding planning books and magazines, and they poured heavy glasses of wine and flipped through the pages, laughing. They'd settled on earth tones, brown and blue and gray.

Memphis sat on the couch, leaning forward, resting his forearms on his knees, as Cincinnati fed him canned pork and beans. He kept his eyes on his fingertips poking out through the top of the salt as he chewed. Pieces of meat stuck in his teeth. He dug at them with his tongue, but they stayed in place. He wished he could stick his pointer finger in his mouth just one last time, lodge the nail between his molars, pull out the tiny pieces of processed meat that felt so large against his gums.

He had been itchy since the surgery. He wasn't sure if it was just in his head, but his whole body felt like a rash. There were no marks on his skin, but it itched and burned on his chest and neck, in his armpits and in between his legs. The worst, though, was at the ends of his stumps. He could feel the skin where the doctor had cauterized his wounds stitching itself back together. Beneath the bandages, he knew, something beautiful was happening. When the scabs dried and flaked off, the new skin would be brighter and pinker than anywhere else on his body.

Cincinnati dipped the spoon into the bowl and lifted the cold mixture to Memphis' mouth. They'd hoped to have a garden established for the next growing season, but it was already too late into the year. They'd tried to plant vegetables, but the rain swelled them to bursting. The time to plant had been weeks before all of this started, back when no one had been affected, back when TVs still worked and airplanes still left trails of exhaust streaking across the sky.

Cincinnati lifted another spoonful to Memphis' mouth. He chewed. He smelled something rotten, but everything stank. The cheap processed pork gave too easily between his teeth, turned to liquid too quickly as he worked it around with his tongue.

·

After the surgery Memphis didn't have the energy to help anyone. He sat in a rocking chair on his front porch, his stumps resting in his lap, turned upward to expose the veins in his forearms. He watched as Cincinnati made rounds through the neighborhood. She listened intently as the survivors spoke, then made notes in her binder. People came to her, showing up on the porch at odd hours. "I woke up and it was like this," an elderly woman in a white nightgown said, holding her head slightly to the side.

Cincinnati leaned in close, pulling apart the woman's hair with her pen. "It does seem off balance," she said.

Memphis thought he could hear a thunderstorm approaching. After a few seconds he realized the sound was not coming from the sky, but from the main road at the entrance to the neighborhood. Other survivors noticed it, too. A man with a bulging pot belly stopped digging a hole in his front yard and stood up straight, jamming the shovel into the ground, shielding his eyes to see better in the high sun.

At the end of the street, the pastor appeared. A golden trumpet hung from his hand. His eyes were open, but his head was tilted forward, looking down at his shoes. He turned and walked up the street, toward the cul-de-sac, into the shadow of the tower.

Behind the pastor, a long line followed closely, two by two, holding hands. The congregation seemed to be pulling the affected along, but it was impossible to tell who was affected and who was not. They all had the same short gait. Their heads all tilted downward at the same angle. Their jaws all clenched tightly, the muscles flexing in their necks and tightening their foreheads.

All other activity on the street stopped. Children dropped their jump ropes and crayons. A woman working under the hood of a rusted brown sedan leaned against the side of the car, the shocks squeaking as her weight transferred to it. More people followed the pastor than Memphis could count, trailing him like the tail of a whip. The pastor led the congregation to the cul-de-sac and they formed a circle around the tower.

"It is faith that has brought us here and faith that will set us free," the pastor said. "I know in my heart that this place is sacred, that these bones do not belong to this earth, that the souls trapped here, reaching to the skies as to the Lord your God, their fingers spread, their mouths open to receive him, are just vessels, and vessels are fragile, and can be broken.

Lord, please forgive us for our proximity to this aberrance, to the rhythm of the waves vibrating right now in our brains and spinal fluid, for the infection of the music and talk radio that we never asked for, that was presented to us at birth, invisible, penetrating the walls of hospital rooms and childhood homes and our mothers' wombs. We did not ask for this burden, God, but please take it from our backs, from our shoulders, from the uneven lumps under our skin, in the curves of our ears."

The pastor lifted the golden trumpet from his side, pointed it skyward, and gave a long, atonal blast. He then turned and walked back toward the end of the street, the congregation close behind him, turning the corner in the direction of the church. Their footsteps faded as evening began to set in, the songs of crickets and frogs filling in the gaps while the survivors stood staring at each other, no one wanting to be the first to move, no one wanting to be the first to make a sound.

·

There were more affected every day. The condition didn't seem to show a preference for children or the elderly, the healthy or the sick. Memphis stopped thinking of the group as survivors. They were all just waiting to take their places in the tower. He sat on the front porch with his stumps in his lap, looking from the bloodstained bandages to the top of the tower and back again, imagining a space for himself up there among the mothers and children, among the neighbors he knew by their faces but never their names.

People whispered stories about the affected. The woman in the wheelchair was affected as she sat watching the birds in the orange trees at the edge of the neighborhood. A father was affected while holding his infant daughter, the young girl's cries waking up the mother. A teenage boy was stricken in the middle of dinner. His family finished off the canned beans on his plate, looking at each other guiltily as they spooned the cold food into their mouths.

The tree surgeon collected them, dragged them to the cul-de-sac, hoisted them into place on the tower, which had by now grown taller than the scaffolding he'd built. Cincinnati oversaw the operation and tried to include Memphis, but his gestures were too easily misunderstood. He watched the construction play out from his porch, discontent, imagining the community growing around him like an ingrown nail.

"We need to consider structural integrity," Cincinnati called up to the tree surgeon as he dangled above her, his safety line tied around the necks and torsos of the affected in the tower. "In a perfect world we'd examine the tower with radar. We'd have worked to a precise blueprint. We should have an idea about how much stress the angles can bear, how high we can reasonably expect the thing to climb, at what point it will start attracting lightning strikes. We don't know any of those things."

The tree surgeon eased the woman in the wheelchair into place, guiding her into a gap that Cincinnati identified from the ground. The tree surgeon rappelled down from the side of the tower, landing with a grunt. "Looks pretty good to me," he said, wiping his hands on his jeans.

Memphis knew they had done their best. The tower was relatively even, though the material they had worked with was irregular. They had balanced the bodies nicely, the young alongside the old, the fat alongside the skinny, the smooth-skinned alongside those covered in patchy hair and insect bites. Cincinnati and the tree surgeon stood side by side, their hands on their hips, looking up at the tower. To Memphis, their heads seemed lifted at an uncomfortable angle. They stood too close to the base of the tower to be able to take it in appropriately. They were only looking at faces and hands from there. It was impossible for them to see the beauty of the whole.

•

Cincinnati had become so pregnant that Memphis thought she might continue swelling until she split open like a watermelon left too long on the vine. They visited the doctor, sitting side by side across the picnic table from her, the blood from Memphis' operation still marring the wood.

"Climb up here," the doctor said to Cincinnati, patting the top of the picnic table. Cincinnati looked over her shoulder, hesitant, before climbing on, but none of the other survivors seemed to care. They had long ago lost their sense of privacy. They sat on their lawns with gardening tools and broken appliances between their feet, showing little interest in productivity. Cincinnati lay flat on the wood. The shadows had shifted. It might already be fall, Memphis realized.

Memphis looked down at Cincinnati. "Count the leaves," he said.

The doctor placed her hands on Cincinnati's belly and pressed against the places where it rose and fell. "When does it move the most?" she asked. "Morning? Evening? Mealtimes?"

Cincinnati looked down at the doctor's hands as they charted the curves of her belly. "It doesn't."

Memphis looked down at the weeds between his feet.

"It doesn't move?" the doctor asked.

"It never has," Cincinnati said. "She never has."

The doctor made a note on a clipboard. "A mother knows certain things," she said, looking at Cincinnati over the top of her notes. Cincinnati nodded.

Between Memphis' feet, the weeds were beginning to flower, yellow and white petals rising above the height that would have been acceptable in the life before everything came apart. He remembered the shame he felt when he forgot to mow his yard, how on weekends the neighborhood would buzz with the sounds of hedge trimmers, how the stretch of sidewalk in front of his little house had been the only stretch of sidewalk on the street where the grass had edged its way onto the concrete, obscuring the clean surface that the other neighbors worked so hard to maintain.

Cincinnati climbed off the table, and she and Memphis made the rounds of the cul-de-sac, noting the mental and physical conditions of the residents, the angles at which they held their heads, their proximity to the tower and the way they looked up at it, unconsciously searching, Memphis assumed, for the faces of their friends and loved ones. There were new additions every day. The tree surgeon had been working so hard, pulling the affected up with his pulley system all alone, that his hands had become swollen and blistered. He stood near the base of the tower, wiping them on his jeans for several minutes, then looking down at them, turning them over, clenching his fists and opening them back up, the movements of his knuckles looking uncomfortable, stiff.

Back on his porch, Memphis looked down at his stumps. The bandages were starting to unravel. He could smell them over the smoke from the bonfires that lined the street. The nights had been getting colder as the afternoon rain became more regular. The survivors sat around the fires looking at each other, trying to predict who would be the next to be affected. It was impossible to tell, and they knew that sooner or later it would be all of them, each and every one, and that all they had worked for would be lost: the stockpiles of food and medicine, the sense of schedule and normalcy, the camaraderie, the battle to keep living rooms and bedrooms clean and free of mud without the help of vacuum cleaners and washing machines. These rooms, they knew, would soon be full of weeds creeping in through cracks around the windows. The cars powering the transmitter would run out of gas. The tall bonfires around which they gathered every night and rekindled every morning would burn down to ash on the pavement, would be extinguished forever by rain, washed away into the storm drains and, eventually, into the ocean.

12

There was no more music in the neighborhood, only the DJ's tired voice, which grew quieter every day. A few days earlier, Cincinnati had taken the CD and record players from him, disassembled them into their component parts and used the pieces to provide more power to the transmitter.

One morning, when the dew seemed to dampen noises from the street, before Cincinnati woke up, Memphis stood over the recliner, listening. The DJ held the microphone so close to his lips he seemed to be kissing its foam cover.

"The smell of loss is in the air. We don't have to worry anymore about traffic accidents, the specter that hung over all of us before this new era, the era of quietude, the time of no sound. How many hours, days of our lives did we waste in anxious stomach-twisting worry about our loved ones, where they were on the roads, how bad the traffic was, et cetera? How many minutes did we pass looking at weather reports, wondering how long it had been since the last rain, how slick the roads would be when our loved ones were on the way home from work? How many seconds ticked by while our eyes were fixed on screens, checking maps and routes, planning ways to avoid other people, ways to cheat the system, to get home a few minutes earlier, to get dinner on the table before sunset, to make sure the kids were bathed and felt loved, to make sure our spouses felt appreciated, to make sure we had the few precious moments we needed to ourselves to maintain our own sanity? Now, we know, none of that matters. The ones we loved are gone, either affected or dead, and the only things we have to replace them are the sounds of crickets and frogs and the multiplying stink of our own bodily fluids. What would you give up to kiss the smooth forehead of your lover one more time? Stay tuned to find out."

The DJ reached for the play button on the CD player, his finger hovering briefly in the air where it had been, but the device was part of the mass of electronics in the living room. There was no room in this new world for art, for music, Memphis now knew. It was an era of extended silences. The DJ had been stripped of his purpose. He had been so in tune with the needs of his listeners, had developed such a keen sense for what song needed to be played before what public service announcement, that he was one of the longest-standing DJs at the radio station. A fixture of the local community, he understood the needs of the people working the graveyard shift, how they craved up-tempo songs that would help them stay awake, how they wanted to hear songs about lost love and the promise of future love, the things that kept them going night after night in the jobs they hated, that kept them driving home as the sun came up, kept them from lying in bed all day as the sun rose and fell and rose again, kept them from the desire to reset their internal clocks, kept them tied so tightly to the cycle of paycheck, bill, paycheck.

•

Cincinnati had stopped keeping track of the food supplies. She sat beside Memphis in a folding chair without making any notes as neighbors came to pick up the canned goods from Memphis' garage. A family of three grabbed cans of beans and corn, looked at her, then back at the diminishing pile, and grabbed more, piling the cans on top of one another, dropping a few as they scurried off. Memphis looked up as a can of pickled beets rolled to the end of the driveway, the sound of metal on concrete loud in the stillness of the early afternoon.

That same afternoon, without Cincinnati to direct the refueling schedule, the cars began running out of gas. One by one, they shut off. The engines clicked for a while as they cooled, and then the street went silent.

The transmitter lost power. The DJ's voice disappeared. In its place, just the wind through the tops of the trees, irregular, low.

Memphis put his stump on Cincinnati's shoulder, shaking her gently, but she stared straight ahead at the house across the street. Memphis stared with her. Before all this, the woman who lived there brought Memphis candied pecans every Christmas. She'd lived alone for years. Memphis couldn't remember when she died. One day there had been cars in her driveway and parked on the street. Family members Memphis had never met stood on the front porch smoking cigarettes in dark suits. They laughed in that quiet way that people do when they know they shouldn't be laughing. After that day the curtains stayed drawn for a long time. Eventually a young couple moved in. Memphis had never spoken to them, and now, they were somewhere near the center of the tower's base. When he'd entered their house, they were together in the bedroom, fully dressed, lying side by side on the bed with their shoes on and their hair neatly styled. They had been holding hands on top of the comforter, not even disturbing the order of the sheets with their bodies. When Memphis led them away from the house and toward the tower, he walked through what was left of their flower bed, stomping down the weeds and the daisies alike.

They continued to sit in silence, Cincinnati gripping Memphis' stump. A gust of wind blew up the street and took loose pages out of her binder, blowing them into the yard and upward, in circles above the driveway, toward the gathering rain clouds in the west.

•

It rained as hard as Memphis could ever remember it raining. The water backed up onto the street and into his yard. He sat next to Cincinnati in the garage as the wind blew rain sideways and onto the slick concrete floor. Cincinnati didn't move when the rain splattered on her face. Her hands curved around the underside of her belly, cradling the lump there. She looked ready to burst, Memphis thought.

Memphis wiped Cincinnati's face dry with his bandaged stump. The healing skin beneath the bandages itched and he wanted to press it into her face, to scratch against her jaw and cheekbones, but he resisted the impulse. He wiped gently, from her forehead down to her lips and over the tops of her eyes. Lightning struck nearby and the thunder rattled the cans of food stacked in the garage. Memphis thought he smelled smoke, lifted his nose to the air, but couldn't tell for sure for sure what it was.

It finally stopped raining close to sunset and Memphis left the garage. He walked out into the street to assess the damage. Folding chairs and patio tables were scattered across lawns. Spanish moss littered the street. The ground was wet and soft and wherever Memphis walked he left footprints that felt deeper than they should have been.

He walked up to the windows of the houses on his street and cupped his stumps around his face to block out the glare from the setting sun. He looked into living rooms, peeking in at the people sitting around coffee tables with candles flickering in the dim light. Their faces were dirty and their hair was tangled. Memphis moved from house to house, checking for signs of life, looking for movement, no matter how slight.

The neighborhood was full of garbage and human waste. Around the time the music stopped, the survivors had grown tired of using the latrine holes and had relieved themselves anywhere they could squat: against trees and bushes, in rain gutters and storm drains. For the first time in a while Memphis could pin the stink down to a function. They had been in a state of suspended decay, and now it was catching up with them. The rain, as it so often did, had sped the process along. Memphis kicked something with his toe and wasn't sure if it was mud or human shit. He turned it over and over with his foot, looking at it, trying to distinguish it from the waterlogged ground, looking for something inside it that might indicate humanity, but he found nothing. It was all just sludge now.

The oak trees in the neighborhood were waterlogged. Memphis could see stains on the bark where the water entered and seeped down toward the ground. They were diseased. Back in some other storm, some hurricane that Memphis couldn't name, the wind had torn limbs off them and left ragged wounds in their place. Scar tissue around the old wounds had allowed elements into the tree that should have been kept out. The trunks, Memphis knew, would be almost hollowed out by rot. They were fragile, but he could only see the signs if he looked close.

As the sun set behind the tall oak trees on the horizon, Memphis heard the familiar shuffle of feet and sat down on the curb, waiting for the procession to reach the neighborhood. This would be the sixth day in a row. Memphis had hardly realized he was counting. The pastor appeared at the end of the street and, again, behind him, the congregation followed, two by two, the survivors leading the affected, though Memphis still couldn't tell which was which. The pastor's head was lowered and Memphis saw the sweat dripping down his cheeks. They marched down the street and into place around the tower. The pastor pointed his golden trumpet at the sky and let loose a long blast.

The wet grass soaked through Memphis' pants. He pulled his knees up to his chest. He could feel the sound waves from the trumpet rattling through the dirt, into his thighs and lower back. He could feel it in his eardrums, like it had changed the air pressure, like everything else was quieter, even though Memphis knew this wasn't true. It was an illusion, like the way that, in the heat of summer, mirages of puddles appeared in the middle of the street, shimmering, rippling, then disappearing.

•

The rain picked up in the middle of the night and continued into the morning. When Memphis woke up it was still thumping against the windows. He pulled back the curtains, and although he knew instinctually that it was morning, the clouds were so thick and dark it looked like dusk. Cincinnati lay in the bed with her eyes open. She hadn't spoken in more than twenty-four hours. Memphis lay back down next to her, put his head on her chest and held his stump against her belly. The bandages were gone now. The ends of his stumps were thick with scabs. He admired them in the strange orange light from the storm. Where the scabs ended on his forearms the new skin was bright pink. He touched the pink skin to his lips and it was soft. It felt like a new finger ready to poke out into the world.

In the living room, the DJ was silent. He stared down at the microphone in his lap, his hands resting limply on the arms of the recliner. He might have been sleeping, Memphis thought, but his eyes were wide open. His breath was measured and slow, and Memphis struggled to hear it over the sound of the rain.

Memphis stood at the window in the living room, looking out onto the street, at the houses they had filled with survivors, houses that had held birthday parties and wakes, houses lined with flowers and painted lovingly by people who had made plans for their lives and eventual deaths. He looked from window to window, watching for curtains to move or another face to appear opposite his. The storm seemed only to get stronger. The wind sounded like a passing train. It had been months now since Memphis had heard a real train, but as the clouds circled overhead he remembered exactly what they'd sounded like, the way they built in the distance and rose to a brief crescendo as they passed by on the way to someplace else, carrying things from one faraway place to another, on predetermined routes, through the middle of swamps and pine stands and out to the coast.

13

When the rain stopped in the afternoon, Memphis went outside and wandered around the neighborhood. There was standing water in the street. Swimming pools overflowed. Potted plants were filled to their brims. When drops fell from the leaves into the bases of the plants, the small waves were enough to crest the pots' edges and splash onto the ground.

Memphis walked around the base of the tower, looking in at the first layer of people, the ones who had lived closest to his house. Their faces were tight and thin. The muscles in their arms were like piano wire. Memphis didn't want to get close enough to see if they were still breathing. It had been so long since they had placed the bodies in the tower. They hadn't fed the affected anything, didn't even know if they could eat. Memphis shook his head and looked up.

The tree surgeon had created something beautiful. The scaffolding was solid. The pulley system twisted slowly in the wind. Memphis had always been bad at estimating distance. He tried to count the layers of bodies to the top of the tower, but they blended together, their open eyes looking the same color, their wet hair plastered down on their heads in the same patterns. It was useless, Memphis realized. He'd never be able to differentiate them again.

Memphis considered knocking on his neighbors' doors, but as he walked to the end of the street he found himself passing the houses without stopping to look inside. He knew what he would find.

Memphis waited at the entrance to the neighborhood. It was almost sunset when the pastor appeared around the corner, his head lowered, his feet sloshing through the floodwater, sending waves out to the curbs on either side of the road. Pieces of paper and tin cans and grass and leaves floated on top of the water, sticking to the pastor's pants, obscuring his feet and shins, making it look like part of him had disappeared into the muck.

Memphis stood in the center of the road, planting his feet in the water. The pastor stopped directly in front of him and looked up from the ground, into Memphis' eyes. "It's time," the pastor said, smiling. "It's been so long coming."

Memphis knew that what they had built was unsustainable, was rotting from the inside as soon as it was set in place. The bodies could never have been a permanent solution. They would grow soft with fungus no matter how many cables Cincinnati hooked to them, no matter how strong their broadcast signal. They were powerless against the decay and they always had been. Memphis nodded.

The congregation encircled the tower. The pastor lifted the trumpet to his lips and gave a long blast. Memphis stood alone by the entrance. A terrible cracking sound came unraveling toward him. He looked up just in time to see limbs falling from the oak trees. Heavy with water, the limbs fractured and fell, their split and pointed ends marring rooftops and piercing lawns, digging trenches in the wet dirt. Memphis watched as, one by one, the biggest limbs broke loose and came to rest on the ground, their odd angles sticking up in the air, the leaves on tiny new branches still fresh and green.

Then the bottom layers of the tower buckled and the upper layers crumbled inward. Memphis heard bones cracking and the sick wet suction of bodies splitting open against the pavement. It sounded like water, the remains of the affected rushing out from the base and down the street. Memphis tried to watch their faces, to remember them, as they fell, but they were too far away, and when they finally reached him it was as a tide of skin and teeth and bone shards swirling in the oily floodwater. And then it was over.

Amid the chaos, the pastor had been leading his congregation back toward the neighborhood's entrance, trudging through the miasma of tangled bodies. Memphis turned to the pastor and held out his stumps, turning them upward so the veins in his wrists were held toward the sky. The pastor reached out and touched the scabs at the end of Memphis' stumps, caressed the pink skin with the tip of a finger.

"If your right hand offends you," the pastor said, "cast it away."

Memphis stepped out of his way and the congregation filed past, two by two, rounding the corner toward the church. Memphis looked at the neighborhood, at the crush of bodies on the ground at the end of the cul-de-sac, and waited for any signs of movement. The sun set and he heard no frogs or crickets. No candles lit up the windows of the houses. The stars came out brighter than Memphis had ever seen.

•

Memphis lay in bed next to Cincinnati. The air was heavy and humid after the rain, and although it was not hot, he found himself sweating into the sheets. Cincinnati stared up at the ceiling without speaking. Memphis rubbed his hand against the lump in her belly. He put his head by her belly button and whispered, "There are so many things to see. The weather doesn't change very much, but it might be fall now and that's the best time of year to be born. You'll feel the cold, but I'll hold you in the sunlight. The rain will stop soon and I'll take you to the beach and we'll look for the horizon line together. The sky will be so clear and blue you won't be able to tell where it meets the water.

"I always wanted to live close to the beach. I liked the idea that things were living right at the edge of where I could swim, just deep enough that I might be able to touch their scales if I were fast enough. I'd hold my breath and dive down and open my eyes in the saltwater and even though it burned I'd keep them open. The water was green and cloudy and I could only see a few feet in front of me, but when I got to the bottom there were shells there, spread out, in colors and shapes I had never seen."

•

In the morning, Memphis wandered among the remains. What was left of the tower was only shin-high and spread out through the entire neighborhood. The night before, he hadn't noticed that some people had been left more or less whole. Memphis knelt down next to the faces of these affected, looking closely at the places where their bodies were open and leaking onto the pavement. He looked at their eyes, but there was no movement in them. Their jaws hung loosely against the ground. Their fingers curled in a way that indicated they were neither open nor closed. He put his cheek next to the mouths of several affected, hoping to feel their breath against his skin, but all he could feel was the breeze from the west.

The dogs showed up and stepped cautiously through the thick pools of blood and organs. They lifted their legs high to cross over the jutting limbs. Memphis tried to scare them away, but there were too many. A large gray dog buried its face in an affected woman's open chest, pulling at the heart exposed by her split-open ribcage. Three more dogs moved in behind him, snatching broken-off fingers and chunks of flesh from heavy thighs. Memphis ran at them, kicking, and the dogs moved far enough away that Memphis couldn't reach them. They growled at him through the meat in their jowls, and in their stares Memphis could see that they understood everything had changed.

•

The DJ might have been breathing but Memphis couldn't tell. He looked briefly at the man, and then at the piano, and then at the box on the coffee table where his hands were buried in salt. He wanted to tip over the box, to spill the bits that had once been attached to him out onto the floor. His fingertips were still there, sticking out from the salt, the nails seeming longer than he remembered, like they had been growing, but that couldn't be possible. He knew it was impossible for them to grow like that, disconnected from his body, without a supply of blood to feed them. Fingernails didn't just grow. They needed a body to anchor them.

He had touched so many things with those fingertips: his own body and others', patterns in stone walls, smooth metal handles on buses and trains, the chipped keys of the piano.

He sat at the bench, in front of the piano, turning his back to the DJ, to the hands, to the pile of leaves in the corner of the living room. He inhaled, lifted his arms, held them out over the keys, and closed his eyes.

It all felt automatic. He remembered where his fingers should land, how the rise and fall of the keys would feel, rounding out the notes, making them complex and necessary. He lowered his arms. Instead of the chord he had been expecting, his stumps pressed the keys without order or pattern, producing a thick ugly sound. Without thinking, he pushed the bench back and stood up, surprised, like he had just seen a snake.

The piano was useless, like so many things. He had never realized before just how useless so many things were. Lawn mowers. Toenail clippers. Alarm clocks.

When Memphis started kicking he didn't have a plan. He kicked with his heel, smashing the bench into splinters. He kicked at the keys, breaking some loose and sending them to the floor. He kicked at the pedals and the legs and the body of the piano. Pieces of wood hit the strings inside, bouncing around, making notes he'd never heard before, a sound like a cancer patient, coughing, coughing, echoing down the hall-ways of the hospital, mixing with the beeping of machines and the whir of ventilators, covered up by the sounds of doctors giving bad news, the sounds of nurses taking meal breaks, the sounds of family members crying softly into their sleeves.

He had lost the music like he had lost so many other things that he had loved or claimed to have loved, and with each kick he felt he was getting it back. His heel kicked through the wood and ached and banged against the hammers and the keys and when Memphis finally stopped and looked down, his legs were cut open and bleeding. The piano leaned to one side but did not collapse. Memphis could see inside it, the guts of the thing exposed. Its mysteries were no longer contained. He'd never be able to tune it again.

•

Memphis sat on the edge of the bed, his pants and shoes covered in dried blood. Cincinnati lay, looking up at the ceiling without blinking, but when Memphis put the end of his stump into her palm she tightened her fingers around his forearm. Memphis pulled and Cincinnati sat up. He led her to the doctor's house.

No one answered when he knocked. Cincinnati stood at his side, her eyes moving but not seeming to register anything. Memphis watched her closely. She looked at the address numbers hung above the door and then at the curtains in the window and then, briefly, at the mess of affected lying in the street where the tower had been, the dogs picking apart the bodies.

Memphis twisted the doorknob between his stumps and the door came open, but the doctor was gone. Her medical bag was on the table, open, but her instruments were missing. He turned around and walked away from the house and out into the street. The floodwater had receded and the pieces of dead grass and trash looked brittle, drying out in the sun. Memphis looked closer at the pavement and noticed a trail of bloody footprints leading away from the doctor's front door and toward the entrance to the neighborhood. The prints were roughly the doctor's size: small, thin. Memphis followed the footprints with his eyes. They glistened and caught the light, still wet. He looked at Cincinnati, at the lump in her belly. They needed medical advice.

Memphis followed the bloody footprints, leading Cincinnati past the other houses, looking into the windows at the survivors. They were all affected. Small families that had made it so far on love and hope were seated around coffee tables, playing cards spread out in front of them, their heads lowered to the floor. The tree surgeon sat in a chair by the window of his house, staring down at his hands in his lap. Memphis could see blisters on the man's palms and the black veins crawling up his wrists and forearms. He pulled and Cincinnati's hand stayed tight around his stump. They started walking toward the edge of the neighborhood, stepping over the corpses spread out in the street and on the sidewalk. Memphis inhaled deeply, smelling the salt in the air, and started following the bloody footprints west toward the coast.

14

The land between Memphis' neighborhood and the coast was a patchwork of planned communities and cow pastures where the development had not yet reached. They walked past rows of houses that were only different from each other in the barest, most superficial ways. Here, a porch with ferns hung on either side of the front door. Here, two columns with twisting patterns that reached to the ceiling. Here, two rocking chairs next to a large window.

They followed the bloody footprints all morning and into the early afternoon. The shadows felt longer, the days felt shorter. They rested in the shade of a low oak tree, its limbs growing sideways out from the trunk, the grass there dead, starved for sunlight. Memphis sat down on an exposed root, pulling Cincinnati down next to him. She knelt automatically but never let go of his forearm.

In the distance, three tall broadcast towers rose up over the tree line. They had once been topped by blinking red lights, warning away passing aircraft, but now they were stark and black against the blue. The house Memphis grew up in was near the base of one of these towers, and his best friend as a child had lived in a small house directly beneath one. The girl's mom, Memphis remembered, had been employed by the TV station. They were supposed to keep trespassers off the land, to keep an eye on the structure, to make sure teenagers didn't climb to the top and have their eyeballs boiled in their skulls by the radio waves.

·

The grass growing through the cracks in the road was waist-high, and the weeds in the roadside ditches were even taller. Memphis looked down at the bloody footprints as he walked along the yellow lines in the middle of the road, between the stopped cars facing either direction. The traffic was orderly. Kids held books in their laps. Passengers looked out windows, resting their chins on their hands, slight smiles on their faces. It had been months, but they looked like they could have been newly affected. The bloody footprints, too, looked fresh, though in the heat of the late afternoon they might have been congealing, the bright red darkening, drying into a thick paste.

The cars were lined up as far as Memphis could see, down straightaways on country roads where he'd have been surprised to see any traffic at all. He was hungry and looked in the windows of the cars for granola bars or packages of crackers, but he couldn't manipulate the door handles with his stumps. The shiny handles slipped off his skin and fell back into place without releasing. Even if he could get into a car, he wondered how he'd open a food wrapper. He could use his teeth, he thought, but he had relied on Cincinnati for that kind of thing. She had worked can openers and cut up bites of meat for him. She had wiped his nose and brushed his hair out of his eyes. She had zipped his pants in the morning and unzipped them in the evening.

Cincinnati's eyes shot from side to side. Her jaw clenched and released. Still, Memphis talked to her and the baby. "Just up here is the spring where I learned how to hold my breath underwater. Seventy-two degrees year-round." He put his stump against Cincinnati's belly and Cincinnati inhaled sharply, like something had pricked her. Memphis looked at Cincinnati's face and kept talking to the child inside her. "We'll have it all to ourselves." They kept walking and Memphis watched Cincinnati closely. Her head bobbed. He couldn't tell if she was nodding or just bouncing as they walked. He made sure to match his gait to hers. Their feet fell almost in unison but not quite. Memphis tried to match her breathing, too, but his lungs were bigger and expanded faster, and when he tried slower breaths he felt dizzy.

•

It was almost evening when the driveway of Memphis' childhood home came into view. His last memory there was of loading the piano into the trailer, pulling away, the house shrinking in the car's side-view mirror. It had been so painful to leave the place where he grew up, knowing he'd been unable to save it. He was too young and couldn't take over the mortgage. The bank had seized the property.

The old home was on a long, thin strip of land that had once been a farm. It sat directly in the center of a cluster of tall oaks that Memphis' father had planted when Memphis was a baby. In scrapbooked pictures he climbed the young trees in his underwear, hanging upside down from their low branches. Now, the lowest branches were twenty feet in the air. Leading Cincinnati down the driveway, he tried to pick out which ones had been his favorites as a child, but it was difficult to remember. Maybe they had grown at unexpected angles or had broken off in a storm.

Several of the windows were broken, and the front door was slightly ajar. Memphis pushed it open. It didn't look like the house had ever been occupied again. It was empty of furniture and smelled like mold. He led Cincinnati into his childhood bedroom and guided her to the place where his bed had been. The carpet was ripped up and the floors were bare concrete. He gently sat her down, leaning against the wall, and then sat beside her. His stomach cramped and turned. The mold stink felt heavy in his chest. He leaned over and put his head on Cincinnati's lap and looked up at her bulging belly. He pressed his face into Cincinnati's thighs and inhaled. The smell of her sweat was so familiar that he closed his eyes. Though the room was empty, in his imagination he could see the bookshelf to his left, the wooden desk at his feet, the ceiling alight with hundreds of glow-in-the-dark stars.

•

Memphis woke up coughing, his chest constricted. He could feel the mold in his nose and mouth and lungs. It had settled into the spaces normally reserved for clean air and mucous. It had displaced something and Memphis felt desperate to achieve balance again.

He stood up in the small room, light-headed, and looked down at Cincinnati. He didn't know if she'd slept. Her eyes were still open. She was still seated upright, leaning against the soggy drywall, looking down at her belly, her hands clasped together just underneath its curve. Memphis tried to remember if he had somehow encouraged her to put her hands together like this, to take the pose of the expectant mother, so statuesque in her posture, but he didn't think he had. Even so, it would be impossible to say. The mold made everything feel disjointed.

Memphis knew they couldn't stay there any longer, but he was very hungry. He led Cincinnati to the kitchen, easing open the cabinets he had once known so intimately, afraid he would find a rat or a snake ready to leap out at him. There was no food. The house had been vacant for too long. Any food had long been carried away by squirrels or raccoons. Memphis gave up and took Cincinnati out into the front yard, then turned around when they reached the last large oak tree. The house was no longer protected from the outside world. It was just part of the landscape.

15

When they made it back to the main road, Memphis had some difficulty distinguishing the bloody footprints from the black asphalt. They had darkened and dried and Memphis could only see them clearly in places where the yellow lines were long and unbroken. Where the lines were interspersed with large sections of unpainted asphalt, he had to move forward on the faith that he would find the footprints again.

Ultimately, following the footprints was easy. They moved forward in a straight line. They never took off down side streets or into neighborhoods or around the large parking lots of the occasional big-box store or grocery store. The footprints never wavered. They were laid with purpose. Memphis found strength in their shape and regularity.

•

By mid-afternoon the vegetation on the side of the road had changed from oak trees to saw palmettos. The ground at the edges of the road was no longer black dirt but loose, white sand. Memphis smelled saltwater. There were no hills and he could only see as far as the next bend in the road. The trees, short, unable to grow tall in the sand, were still big enough to block his view. The road curved and suddenly the smokestacks of the coal-burning power plant rose up in front of them. The plant was on the water, built into a natural inlet, and had once pumped saltwater in and out through huge pipes. The smokestacks were stained with decades of soot, but they no longer spit smoke.

The footprints were still there, and Memphis had been watching them so closely that he had become familiar with their small imperfections. This was someone, he had come to realize, who walked awkwardly, balancing their weight on the outsides of their feet. He tried to remember if he had ever noticed the way the doctor walked, if she might have had a slight limp to the left or the right, but it was no use. The things people had done were flushed from his memory. The ways they spoke and smiled seemed like mean tricks now that they were gone.

The estuary at the power plant had been developed into a park after manatees had discovered the unnaturally warm water from the cooling pipes. The huge creatures would gather in the shallow water, protected from boats, and people would stand on wooden piers looking down at the wide gray shapes floating almost motionless in the water. As Memphis and Cincinnati approached the park, informational placards lined the walkway. The bloody footprints led out past the wide-open grassy area once used for picnics, toward a seawall built from chunks of concrete. In the distance, Memphis could make out a human figure in the water, about waist deep. He slowed down and looked at Cincinnati. Her breath came in small, shallow gulps. He had been so focused on the footprints that he hadn't noticed this change. Her eyes were narrow, pinched, as though she was in pain. She kept one hand, protectively, on the center of her stomach, covering her belly button.

As they got closer to the figure in the water, Memphis could see it was the doctor. She was bent over at the waist, working intently on something beneath the surface, struggling, pulling. Suddenly, her arm came free and rose from the water. Holding something black and oblong, she turned and headed back to the shore. She dropped the object onto a pile of similarly shaped objects and turned to face Memphis. "How did you find me?" she asked.

Memphis gestured at the ground, where the trail of bloody footprints led across the grass and out into the water. The doctor started to weep.

"They have hands just like we do," she said, wiping snot from her nose. "The bones are in there and everything. They have thumbs. They have knuckles. It's just covered over by skin. It's thick but it's just skin."

Memphis looked out at the water at the rounded shapes of what he thought might be manatees. He squinted to see better. The sun was heading toward the horizon and glared in his eyes. There were dozens of them out there, floating peacefully, even more than he'd ever seen when the power plant had been operational. The power plant hadn't been pumping warm water into the bay for months. They had gathered here anyway, longing for a time they somehow understood was gone.

Manatees move slowly, which is why their backs were so often disfigured by boat propellers. They simply couldn't get out of the way fast enough, but they did move. The shapes out in the water, however, didn't appear to be moving with any kind of purpose. They bobbed like seaweed on the small waves that came in through the mouth of the inlet. Memphis squinted his eyes tighter, feeling as if it would help him make out his surroundings.

The water was tinted red. As it lapped at the white sand it left behind red foam that deformed slightly when the breeze caught it. Memphis looked down at the doctor's clothes. Her white coat was pink with blood.

"It's only just skin that's keeping them together," she said, "that's keeping us together. It's only skin. It's just skin. It's an organ. Did you know that? It keeps the outside out."

Memphis shook his head. There was too much blood in the water. The manatees weren't moving slowly. They weren't moving at all.

•

Cincinnati's contractions started late in the night. The doctor built a small fire on the beach and placed the severed manatee flippers into it, one by one. Memphis thought she might cook them, but instead she simply watched as they blistered and cracked, then placed another one on top. There must have been meat on them, Memphis thought. He was so hungry.

The doctor measured Cincinnati's contractions by her grunts. She still wasn't speaking. She lay back on the sand and bore down at regular intervals: fifteen minutes apart, then ten, then seven.

"It's coming," the doctor said. "She'll be here soon."

Memphis knelt in the sand by Cincinnati's side and cradled the back of her head in the crook of his elbow. "Push," he said when the doctor looked up at him from between Cincinnati's legs. "Rest," he said when the doctor looked up at him again. Cincinnati seemed to be listening. She pushed and rested in the precise pattern that she needed to. Memphis wasn't sure if he was helping, but saying the words made him feel useful in a way he hadn't for a long time. The doctor had her hand inside Cincinnati, feeling for the baby's head. Memphis couldn't have guessed how long she labored. It was dark and the fire kept dying down. The doctor put more driftwood on top, and more manatee flippers, and it smelled like charred meat all night.

Finally, just as the sun was coming up behind them, to the west, over the swamps and the pine stands and the oak forests that stretched back in the direction they'd come, the direction, Memphis knew, they'd never be able to go again, the baby came out of Cincinnati like a clog clearing a drain: all at once, with great force. The doctor caught her and cut the umbilical cord and handed her to Memphis.

The little girl was wet with blood and afterbirth and, in the first light of morning, she seemed to shine with all the brightness of the sun.

Memphis put his face next to hers, trying to tell if she was breathing. He placed the scabbed end of his stump on her belly, hoping to feel it was rising and falling, but he couldn't tell, he couldn't tell, he couldn't tell. The doctor knelt over Cincinnati, wiping her forehead with a bloodstained rag. "It's all over," Memphis heard her whispering. "You can rest now."

Memphis held the little girl up into the light and looked at her closely. She was perfect. Her little hands were balled into tight fists. Memphis counted her limbs and digits: all there. Her eyes were shut. He stumbled down toward the water and fell to his knees, holding the little girl against his chest, weak, exhausted. The tide was out and the corpses of manatees littered the beach. The places where their flippers had been were now just holes. Small waves nudged their bodies forward, forward, farther onto the shore.

Photo © Kara Hoyt

ABOUT THE AUTHOR

Shane Hinton is the author of the story collection *Pinkies* and editor of the anthology *We Can't Help It If We're From Florida*. He teaches writing at the University of Tampa and lives in the winter strawberry capital of the world.

ACKNOWLEDGEMENTS

Special thanks to: Meredith Alling, Kristen Arnett, John Brandon, Brock Clarke, Erica Dawson, Asha Dore, Jess, Further, Vera, Iris, Mikhail Iossel, Jason Ockert, Jeff Parker, Steph Post, Ryan Rivas, George Singleton, Lidia Yuknavitch.

SUBSCRIBE

We thrive on the direct support of enthusiastic readers like you. Your generous support has helped Burrow, since our founding in 2010, provide over 1,200 opportunities for writers to publish and share their work.

Burrow publishes four, carefully selected books each year, offered in an annual subscription package for a mere $60 (which is like $5/month, $0.20/day, or 1 night at the bar). Subscribers are recognized by name in the back of our books, and are inducted into our not-so-secret society: the illiterati.

Glance to your right to view our 2019 line-up. Since you've already (presumably) read *this* book, enter code **RADIO25** at checkout to knock 25% off this year's subscriber rate:

BURROWPRESS.COM/SUBSCRIBE

VENUS IN RETROGRADE
poetry by Susan Lilley

$20 | Hardcover | 136 pages

In a voice both lyrical and conversational, Lilley interprets various stages of womanhood while parsing the beauty and decay of her beloved homestate of Florida.

RADIO DARK
a novel by Shane Hinton

$16 | Paperback | 140 pages

Somewhere in Florida, where the sprawling suburbs meet a dying citrus grove, a janitor at a small community radio station, an FCC field agent, and a DJ attempt to restore humanity to a fallen world.

BRIGHT LIGHTS, MEDIUM-SIZED CITY
a novel by Nathan Holic

$25 | Hardcover | 620 pages
+ comic panels & watercolor illustrations

In the spirit of city novels like Tom Wolfe's *The Bonfire of the Vanities*, this sprawling period piece follows a hopeless house-flipper caught amid the 2009 housing bubble in Orlando, FL.

BONUS BOOK ARTIFACT
in collaboration with Obra/Artifact

For subscribers only. A limited edition book-as-object created in partnership with Stetson University's MFA-run literary journal, Orba/Artifact.

the illiterati

Florida isn't known as a bastion of literature. Being one of the few literary publishers in the state, we embrace this misperception with good humor. That's why we refer to our subscribers as "the illiterati," and recognize them each year in our print books and online.

To follow a specific publishing house, just as you might follow a record label, requires a certain level of trust. Trust that you're going to like what we publish, even if our tastes are eclectic and unpredictable. Which they are. And even if our tastes challenge your own. Which they might.

Subscribers support our dual mission of publishing a lasting body of literature and fostering literary community in Florida. If you're an adventurous reader, consider joining our cult—er, cause, and becoming one of us...

One of us! One of us! One of us!

2019 illiterati

Park Ave CDs
Secret Society Goods
Emily Dziuban
Linda Buckmaster
Robert Veith
Pam Escarcega
Randi Brooks
Lauren Salzman
Drew Hoffmann

Michael Wheaton
Kristen Arnett
Cindy & Frank Murray
Naomi Butterfield
Ted Greenberg
Gene Albamonte
Vicki Entreken
Cooper Levey-Baker
Whatever Tees

Nayma Russi
Lauren Mitchell
Roberta Alfonso
Terry Godbey
Mary T. Duerksen
Debbie Goetz
Mary Reed
Grover Austin
Paula Bowers
Jean Dowdy
Stephen Cagnina
Yana Keyzerman
Amy Suzanne Parker
Jonathan Fink
Brian Turner
Joe McGee & Jess Rinker
Kim Britt
Martha Brenckle
John Henry Fleming
Thomas M. Bunting Projects
Jane Trimble & Robert Ambes
Rebecca Evanhoe
Adam C. Margio
Joshua Moye
Kelly Schumer
Jason Holic
Hunter Choate
Erica McCay
Shelby Nathanson
J. Thomas Wright
John & Pam Holic
Aaron & Patti Holic
Susan Scrupski
Catherine Carson

Mary Ann de Stefano
Michelle Riddle
Michael Gualandri
Richard Varner
Victoria Webster-Perez
Peter M. Gordon
Bonnie Frenkel
Jean West
NM Greenberg
Jason Katz
J.C. Carnahan
Pamela Melear
Patty Daoust
Marc Vaughan
Lisa Hinton
Chuck Dinkins
Tania Parada
Dystacorp Light Industries
Emily Webber
Abigail & Henry Craig
Jeanan Davis
Matthew Lang
Courtney Clute
Michael Cuglietta
Anna
Virginia Beeson
Mistie Watkins
The Taitts
Paul L. Bancel
Martha Sarasua
Jeff Ferree
Barbara Van Horn
Benjamin Noel
Pat Rushin

Sara Isaac
Nancy Pate
Amy Letter
Rita Ciresi
Dirt Dog Dustin
Alissa Barber Torres &
Anthony Torres
Heather Owens
Alicia Marini
Peter Bacopoulos
Lora Waring
Giti Khalsa
Chris Wiewiora
Travis Kiger
pete !
Alexandra Mariano
Erich Schwarz
Alison Townsend
Kim Rose
Neil & Sarah Asma
Valerie & Ross Blakeslee
A John Gosslee
Martin Fulmer
Dainon Moody
J. Stroup
Robert Lipscomb
Irene L. Pynn
Libby Ludwig
Amy Copeland
Kimberly Lojewski

Amy Copeland
Rebecca Renner
Chrissy Kolaya
Alison Jennings
Elena Postal
Anonymous
Suzannah Gilman
Blaine Strickland
Danielle Kessinger
Melanie
Margaret Nolan
Erin Hartigan
Stuart Buchanan
RC Wahl
Georgia Parker
Jackie Pappas
David James Poissant
Stacey Matrazzo
Nikki Fragala Barnes
Stacy Barton
Cindy Simmons
Sarah Hicks
Chelsea Torregrosa &
Matthew H. Bowlin
David Lilley
Spencer Orenstein
Ciarra Johnson
Cristina Wright
Lucianna Chixaro Ramos